"Wes, meet Audra." She held the infant out to him. **"Please help me."**

The weight of Audra in his arms made her all the more real. Her cries stopped as a soft mew emanated from the tiny bundle. He didn't want to look. But he couldn't not look. He needed to see his daughter.

"Oh, my God." His heart sprang back to life.

"What is it?" Jade frantically asked.

"She's beautiful," he whispered.

"They all are. We made quite the heartbreakers."

He lifted his gaze to hers. The edginess had faded to a gentle softness. Even with her stained blouse and what appeared to be a black marker streak across her left cheek, she exuded beauty. "I guess we did." He lowered his eyes to the other two girls contentedly sucking on the bottles Jade held for them.

And then he saw more black marker. "Did you write on their feet?"

Dear Reader,

Welcome to the fourth book in my Saddle Ridge, Montana series! *The Bull Rider's Baby Bombshell* came together during one of my "thinking" car rides. Most of my brainstorming occurs on the road alongside Duffy—my four-legged sidekick. The changing scenery never fails to spark ideas. When I drove past a woman pushing one of those three-across triplet strollers down the main street of a little country town, Wes and Jade's story immediately began churning in my brain.

I love characters who share a past, but not necessarily a romantic one. And Wes and Jade's acrimonious history definitely gives them reason to keep their distance from one another...until they find themselves temporarily parenting six-week-old triplets.

I've always envisioned actress Kat Dennings as Jade Scott. Her take-no-prisoners attitude is a perfect match for a stubborn Slade man. And when I first saw fitness model Parker Hurley astride a steel horse in the pages of a fashion magazine, I knew he was my Wes.

I hope you enjoy *The Bull Rider's Baby Bombshell*. Feel free to stop in and visit me at amandarenee.com. I'd love to hear from you.

Happy reading!

Amanda Renee

THE BULL RIDER'S BABY BOMBSHELL

Amanda Renee

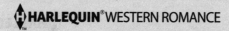

Recycling programs
for this product may
not exist in your area.

ISBN-13: 978-1-335-69968-8

The Bull Rider's Baby Bombshell

Copyright © 2018 by Amanda Renee

Printed in U.S.A.

www.Harlequin.com

Amanda Renee was raised in the northeast and now wriggles her toes in the warm coastal Carolina sands. Her career began when she was discovered through Harlequin's So You Think You Can Write contest. When not creating stories about love and laughter, she enjoys the company of her schnoodle, Duffy, as well as camping, playing guitar and piano, photography and anything involving animals. You can visit her at amandarenee.com.

Books by Amanda Renee

Harlequin Western Romance

Saddle Ridge, Montana

The Lawman's Rebel Bride
A Snowbound Cowboy Christmas
Wrangling Cupid's Cowboy

Harlequin American Romance

Welcome to Ramblewood

Betting on Texas
Home to the Cowboy
Blame It on the Rodeo
A Texan for Hire
Back to Texas
Mistletoe Rodeo
The Trouble with Cowgirls
A Bull Rider's Pride
Twins for Christmas

Visit the Author Profile page
at Harlequin.com for more titles.

For Brad.

Thank you for the inspiration.

Chapter One

Call Jade.
I can't do this.
Please forgive me.

Jade Scott read her sister's note for the tenth time since arriving in Saddle Ridge. Almost an entire day had passed since Liv had vanished, leaving behind her month-and-a-half-old triplets. Jade would've arrived sooner if there had been more flights out of Los Angeles to the middle-of-nowhere Montana. She'd ditched the godforsaken town eleven years ago and had sworn never to return. But her sister's children had annihilated that plan. Especially since Jade had been partially responsible for their existence.

"I didn't call the police like you asked, but now that you're here, I think we should."

"No!" Jade spun to face Maddie Winters, her sister's best friend and the woman who had taken care of the children for the past twenty hours. "As soon as we do, Liv's labeled a bad parent and those girls go in the system."

"Nobody will take them away with you here." Maddie checked to see if there were any new messages on her phone. "I'm really worried about her."

Jade scanned the small living room. A month ago, it looked like a baby—or three—lived there. Today it looked cold and sterile, devoid of any signs of the triplets. The crocheted baby blankets and baskets of pastel yarn were gone from the corner. Once covered with stacks of photo albums her sister couldn't wait to fill, the coffee table now sat bare. Embroidered pillows with their cute mommy and baby sayings no longer littered the couch. Her sister had even removed the framed pictures of the girls along with their plaster hand- and footprints from the mantel. Except for the video baby monitor, nothing baby related remained in sight. Why? She knew Liv's desire for order was strong thanks to their chaotic upbringing, but she'd never thought her sister would wipe away all visible traces of her children.

"I'm worried too. We don't need to involve the police though. She wasn't kidnapped." Liv was a chronic planner and everything about the situation felt deliberate. "She made a conscious decision to walk away. She wrote a note, she called you to babysit and then left on her own accord. If we call the police, the girls go into the system. Hell will freeze over before I let that happen."

Jade knew all about the system. She and Liv had spent fourteen years in foster care, bounced from place to place until Liv had been old enough to become her guardian. Being two teenage girls on their own had forced them to grow up fast. Too fast.

Jade's phone rang inside her bag jarring her back to the present. It wasn't her sister's ringtone, but she reached for it to be safe. It was her office in Los Angeles. She answered, praying Liv had called there by mistake instead of her cell and they were patching the call over to her. "Yes."

"I'm sorry to bother you," Tomás, her British assistant, began. "I just wanted to let you know the Wittingfords have finally decided on their venue for their summer opener."

Jade's heart sank. Tomás's call was great news, just not the news she wanted to hear at that moment. The Wittingfords were the most extravagant clients her event planning company had seen to date. And their show-stopping party guaranteed to outshine all the celebrity weddings she'd produced this year.

"I'm glad to hear it. I just wish I was there to oversee it." Jade tugged her laptop out of her bag and opened it on the dining room table. "Email me the contract and I'll review it. I want you to look it over first. Flag anything you question. I need you to be my extra set of eyes while I'm away. And please call my clients and tell them I've had a family emergency. Give them your contact info and make sure they understand I haven't abandoned them. But they need to phone you with any issues or changes and you can fill me in later."

"I'll get on it, straightaway. Any news about your sister?"

"Nothing yet." Jade lifted her gaze to see Maddie glaring at her from the living room. "I need to go. We'll talk later."

"I can't believe you're putting work first." Maddie picked up the baby monitor from the coffee table and checked the screen.

"I'm sorry you don't approve of my multitasking." Jade turned on the computer. "I know my sister. She doesn't do crazy. Wherever she is, I'm sure she's safe. While I try to figure out what's going on with her and where she ran off to, I still have a business to maintain."

"And walking out on your newborn triplets isn't crazy?"

Not unless you knew the whole situation. "All right, tell me again. What time did you come over yesterday afternoon?"

"A little after three. Liv sounded frazzled when she called. I asked what was wrong, but she kept doing that answer a question with a question thing that drives me up a wall. I got nothing out of her." Maddie ran both hands through her hair, on the verge of tears. "I tried to talk to her, but she took off the second I walked in. I found the note taped to the nursery room door a few minutes after that."

"When did she remove the baby things from in here?"

"I don't know." Maddie shook her head wildly. "I'm trying to remember the last time I came over."

"What do you mean? You're her best friend and you didn't check on her? When I left, you assured me you would. You only live next door."

"She insisted on space so she could learn how to take care of the girls on her own. I guess it's been a little over a week since I've been here. I'll be honest, her abrupt dismissal hurt. I had been staying in the guest room after you left. I should have noticed something was wrong."

Uneasiness grew deep within Jade's chest. "I keep thinking the same thing. I missed our video chat on Sunday night because I was too busy with work." Many of Jade's ex-boyfriends had accused her of putting her career before anyone else. Had she selfishly done the same with her sister? Jade scanned her inbox, hoping to find an email from Liv. Nothing. "I'll check her office. Are you able to stay for a little while longer?"

"For however long you need."

Jade continued to walk around the old farmhouse. Her sister had set up three bassinets in the room next to her office in addition to an equal number of cribs in the former master bedroom, now the nursery. Liv had been prepared. Some may even say overprepared. She'd read every parenting book and magazine she found. Took infant care classes and had insisted Jade learn infant CPR too. From researching the best laundry detergents and baby shampoos to memorizing the symptoms of childhood illnesses and diseases, she'd planned for every contingency. It didn't make sense why she left. Outside of neither of them not knowing what good parenting was.

Their father had been a drifter and their mother had been behind bars on and off since Jade was two. They'd seen the inside of more foster homes than they could count. Some good, some bad. Whenever they had made it into a decent one, their mother had gotten out of jail, claimed to be ready to raise them again after completing her therapy and halfway house program only to fail miserably weeks later and wind up right back in jail. Her mother had always wanted what she couldn't have. That included Liv and Jade. Once in her care, she'd discovered they were too much work to support. Besides, her drugs were more important. She wanted those more than anything. More than her children.

The court system had reached a point where they said no more, and Jade and Liv had mixed emotions the day they learned they wouldn't have to live with their mother ever again. Liv had handled it better than she had. Jade had been angry. All the time. It hadn't helped that kids had picked on her constantly at school. One kid had been the ringleader. The one she had trusted, and then he betrayed her. And she had never forgotten him. Wes Slade.

Jade opened the bottom filing cabinet drawer and scanned the hanging folder tabs. The last one had *BABY* scrawled on it. The generic word surprised her. At the very least, she'd expected all three girls' names to be written on the label, if not three separate files. She removed the thick folder, laid it on the desk and began looking through it. On top was the first ultrasound picture of the triplets. Jade ran her fingers over the black-and-white image. She could still see her sister holding up the photo to the screen during their video chat. Liv had been shocked, but thrilled just the same. She was finally getting the family she had always wanted. And it had been a long time coming.

Liv had battled fertility issues for years. Married at twenty-three, she and her husband had tried everything to get pregnant. There was just enough wrong with each of them to prevent a successful pregnancy. Kevin had wanted to adopt, but it had been important to Liv to carry her children and have a physical connection to them. He'd refused the donor idea and their constant baby battles wound up destroying their marriage.

Jade sat in Liv's ultralux, oversize perfect-for-pregnancy office chair and glanced around the room. Her sister had always been neat and organized. Not a pen or paperclip out of place. She peered inside Liv's desk drawers hoping to find a clue to her whereabouts. Everything related to her job as a financial planner. Liv still had another two months of maternity leave until she had to return to work full-time. Working from home would help the transition although Liv had considered hiring a nanny during the day so she could talk to clients without interruption.

Her sister had a plan. A definitive plan on how her life would run smoothly as a single mom of three children. Walking away was completely out of character.

Jade continued to flip through the contents of the folder. The only item left was Jade's egg donation contract giving her sister the biological link to the babies she wanted. She just hadn't expected Liv to use all the embryos at once. Because of her sister's long infertility battle, the doctor had believed her best chance for a successful pregnancy was to implant them all in hopes one would survive. The surprise had been universal.

"Dammit, Liv, where are you?"

She stood to put the folder back in the drawer when she noticed another one lying on the bottom of the cabinet. Sliding the other files forward, she removed the thin, unmarked and probably empty folder. She flipped it open to double-check and saw another donor contract. Why? Jade had been the only donor. Liv had used a fertility clinic for the father.

She began to read the document:

This agreement is made this 22 day of July 2017, by and between Olivia Scott, hereafter RECIPI-ENT, and Weston Slade, hereafter DONOR.

"No, no, no!" Jade's heart pounded in her chest. "Liv couldn't have." She continued to read the contract. But she had. Wes Slade was the donor and the father of Jade's biological children. Her sister had fertilized Jade's eggs with the man she despised more than anyone.

A FEW HOURS LATER, Jade stood in front of the check-in clerk at the Silver Bells Ranch lodge. The woman whispered into the phone. "One of Wes's fans is here to see him."

"Excuse me. I am no fan of his."

The clerk cupped the mouthpiece and whispered, "She may be an ex-girlfriend."

"Are you kidding me?" Jade reached over the counter and snatched the phone. "This is Jade Scott. I need to speak to Wes concerning my sister, Liv. It's…um… an emergency of sorts."

Still reeling from her discovery, Jade needed absolute confirmation Wes was the triplets' father. She prayed he had backed out or that Liv had changed her mind at the last second. Anything…just not this.

"Oh hey, Jade. It's Garrett, Wes's brother. It's been what, ten years or more? I saw your sister and the triplets last week. They sure are beautiful. Reminded me of my two when they were born."

You have no idea. Jade swallowed hard. "I'm staying with the kids for a few days while Liv is—is away on business. She's unreachable today and I have a problem at the house. Since she and Wes are friends, I'm thinking he might have some ideas." At least Jade assumed they were friends. Who would ask a casual acquaintance to father their children?

"He's out with our guests on a trail ride. He should be back soon. You're welcome to wait or maybe I can help you."

"Uh, um. No. I appreciate the offer, but I need Wes. I don't mind waiting." Yeah, she did. The longer she waited, the more questions churned in her brain. "Where's the best place I can catch him?"

"The stables." Garrett paused. "Do you have the girls with you? I'm sure my daughter would love to me—"

"They're with the sitter." The last thing Jade needed was to introduce the triplets to their cousin.

The entire time Liv had been pregnant, Jade kept her part in the process tucked neatly away in the dark recesses of her brain. Surprisingly, Liv had carried to almost thirty-seven weeks. The day of her sister's scheduled cesarean, Jade had been by her side in the operating room, cheering her on. But the moment Jade had held those tiny bundles of perfection and stared into their blue eyes, reality hit. She was the biological mother of three little girls and she had wrestled with it during the rest of her stay in town. They were Liv's children. Not hers. It wasn't until she was on a plane flying back to LA three weeks later that she finally breathed easier. Once she had returned to her normal routine, any lingering thoughts of being their mother faded and she gladly slipped into the role of auntie.

Until today.

She needed to find Liv…fast.

GARRETT TOOK THE reins as Wes dismounted. "Thanks for helping out."

"No problem." Wes didn't mind filling in for other employees while he was visiting the ranch, considering they had covered for him plenty during his last few months of employment on Silver Bells. It had been an unbearable period in his life and he'd wanted nothing more than to get away from Saddle Ridge. And he had. He'd moved to Texas and escaped the drama he once called home.

"Oh, I almost forgot." Garrett snapped his fingers. "You have a visitor. Do you remember Jade Scott?"

Wes damn near tripped at the mention of her name. Even though he couldn't think of one person he despised more than Jade, it was her sister he didn't want to think about.

"What is she doing here?"

"I guess she's babysitting the triplets while her sister's away on business. She has some emergency at

Liv's house. I offered to help, but she insisted on talking to you."

"Keep your distance from the Scotts." Wes swallowed hard. This was exactly why he hadn't wanted to come home for his brother Dylan's wedding and his niece and nephew's christenings. "They can call someone else. I have no business with Liv or Jade."

"What's with the attitude?" Garrett asked. "I thought you and Liv were good friends. Besides, it's too late. Jade's about ten steps behind you."

Wes turned to see her weaving through the ranch guests walking back to the lodge. His stomach somersaulted at the sight of her and he wasn't sure if it was because of their past or how much she had transformed since high school. The mean girl who had once made his life miserable had gone from a rough, chip-on-her-shoulder teen to a California knockout.

Sleek, rich mahogany waves replaced the frizzy curls she used to have. But that body and those curves…good Lord Almighty! Her black polka-dot chiffon blouse revealed just enough of her ample cleavage to make any man look twice, and her tailored black pants hugged her hips in perfection. She exuded an edginess combined with old Hollywood glamour and if she had been any other woman on the planet, he would have moved in for the kill. Their past made her off-limits and his connection to her sister sealed that deal.

"Wes." Deep blue eyes held his gaze before traveling the length of him and back.

Transfixed upon her matte ruby-red lips, it took every ounce of strength he had left to respond. "Jade."

"Hey, kids. A conversation requires more than that." Garrett laughed. "Try hello, how are you." He nudged his brother in Jade's direction before walking away.

"What do you want?" Wes hadn't meant his tone to be as harsh as it sounded.

"It's about Liv. Is there someplace private we can talk?"

Wes stiffened. "I have work to do." He turned to tend to his horse, but it wasn't there. Silently, he cursed his brother.

"I thought you were on vacation from your job in Texas."

He reeled to face her. "Who told you that?"

"The rodeo school where you work." She stepped toward him and wobbled in her ranch-inappropriate four-inch heels. He reached for her arm to steady her and instantly regretted the contact. "I looked you up online. I need your help."

Wes released her and rubbed his palm, wanting to erase all traces of her from his body. "On second thought, I don't care what your reasons are. I'm asking you as politely as possible to leave."

"Wes, please." A half-foot shorter, even in those ridiculous heels, she stared up at him.

"What could you possibly need my help with?"

"Tell me I can trust you first."

"No. You can't trust me, so let's end this now. Goodbye, Jade." The intoxicating scent of her perfume wasn't enough to entice him to hear more.

"I know."

It wasn't so much the words, but the firm way she

said them that stopped him in his tracks. "Do you care to expand on that?" He prayed it wasn't what he thought.

"I found the contract today at my sister's house," Jade whispered. "Before I go into details, promise me everything I tell you will stay between us."

Wes wanted to argue and deny his role in Liv's daughters' paternity, but the worry etched into Jade's face gave him pause. "Okay, you have my attention. And yes, you can trust me."

Jade assessed him sharply, making him more uncomfortable than he already was. She had no reason to take him at his word considering their past had thrived on a mutual loathing of one another after their brief high school romance. Her shoulders sagged as she closed her eyes momentarily, shielding him from the pain that reflected in them.

"Liv left the triplets with Maddie yesterday and hasn't returned."

"That doesn't sound like Liv." Wes's heart dropped into his stomach. "Have you called the police? Or checked the hospitals?"

"I called every hospital within a two-hundred-mile radius while I waited for my flight last night. I don't want to involve the police. This isn't a case of her getting in a car accident. She left a note saying she was leaving. Do you have any idea where she might've gone? Has she ever mentioned a place she enjoyed going to when she was under a lot of stress or anywhere she always wanted to visit?"

"Not offhand. I can't believe she left the girls." Wes propped a booted foot up on the fence rail and stared into the corral. "I was afraid this would be too much for her."

"Wait a minute." Jade grabbed him by the arm and forced him to look at her. "You suspected she was in trouble?"

"That's not what I'm saying." Wes checked over his shoulder to make sure they were still alone. "I was long gone before those babies were born. And for the record, this wasn't an easy decision on my part. There was never anything romantic or sexual between your sister and me. We were good friends. She was there for me during the darkest time of my life."

"So how did you get from point A to point B?" Her face soured. "She told me she used an anonymous donor."

"Liv hated the thought of a stranger fathering her children. I had initially said no, then I realized she wanted this more than anything and relented. I felt I owed her for being there for me over the years. But that's where it ended. I couldn't continue our friendship, knowing she was carrying my—" Wes shook his head. "They are not my children. I refuse to say they are."

"I'm not asking you to raise them." Thick sarcasm laced her assurance. "Just tell me what happened."

Wes hesitated before answering, not wanting to sound callous. "Liv and I went our separate ways. She called me once I was in Texas and told me she was having triplets. I'll admit, I had my concerns and asked if she could handle that many babies. She said she was a little overwhelmed by the news, but even more excited. I could hear it in her voice. She also had you and her friends. So, I continued on with my life."

"Turns out she was more overwhelmed than we both thought." Jade's phone rang. She removed it from her bag, checked the screen and then rejected the call. "No matter how long it takes to find her, I'm not abandoning those babies. You can't, either."

"I am not getting involved. I did my part and then got out of town for a reason. Many reasons. They are not my responsibility. She should have gone with an anonymous donor like she had with the eggs."

"She didn't use an anonymous egg donor."

"Then whose were they?"

"Mine. You and I are those girls' biological parents."

Chapter Two

Jade never saw a person pale so fast. "Don't you dare faint on me."

"For God's sake, I've never fainted a day in my life. A bull has knocked me unconscious a time or two in the rodeo ring, but I've never fainted." Wes's hazel eyes narrowed. "You're the biological mother of those children?"

"Believe me, when I saw your name on the donor contract I was none too thrilled. It's like the universe was playing some cruel joke on me."

"On you?" Wes snapped. "You're the last person I would have chosen." His abhorrence for her darkened his features. Features she probably would've found attractive under normal circumstances.

"At least I provided a biological link. You, on the other hand—"

"Go on. Finish what you were going to say." The muscles along his jawline pulsated.

"No, because regardless of our feelings toward each other, we created three beautiful lives. I will not insult them by insulting you."

Wes tilted his hat back, revealing an errant lock of

dark blond hair. He folded his arms across his chest, causing his formfitting gray T-shirt sleeve to ride up and expose the hint of a colorful tattoo on his biceps. Biceps that were much larger than she remembered from high school.

"As much as I want to argue with you, that's a very mature attitude and one I should adopt myself." Wes stepped away from the fence, giving her his full attention. "When I agreed to do this, I did so under one condition. Total anonymity."

"I have no intention of saying anything." Jade had wanted the same condition, but she and Liv had discussed the possibility of one day telling the children. Especially if a medical reason arose. That was most likely why she wanted the father to be somebody she knew. Just in case. "The truth may come out, regardless."

"It can't." Wes's eyes widened. "I had second thoughts shortly after I did it. First of all, I never wanted kids of my own. And second, my family would never forgive me for not being involved in their lives. Even though that's what Liv wanted."

"Yeah, I'm not so sure about that." Jade wondered if her sister's feelings for Wes ran deeper than she'd admitted. "Had you already planned to move away when she asked you to be the donor?"

"No. I mean, we discussed how unhappy I was living in Saddle Ridge for reasons I won't get into right now. My bull riding schedule keeps me on the road a lot too, so she knew I wouldn't be around much."

"How did she react when you told her you were moving to Texas?"

Wes winced and rubbed the back of his neck. "I told her over the phone after I had already left. It was all of a two-minute conversation. One I purposely kept short because I couldn't handle being involved in her pregnancy or the baby's life. Then she called and told me she was having triplets."

"You had to have been as shocked as I was." The thought of Liv carrying and raising one of Jade's children had been surreal enough. And even though she'd been fully aware they'd harvested three of her eggs, Jade never saw beyond one child. She'd automatically assumed it was a one-time deal. At the very least she'd expected her sister to have told her they'd used all three the day of the procedure.

"That's an understatement. Look, I just came off a full week of competition and I'm only here for another week and a half before I head back to Texas. My family has two baby christenings this weekend and Dylan's wedding is the next. And I'm competing midweek in South Dakota. I'll help you in whatever way I can, but I'm not going anywhere near those babies. I can't do it. Despite what you think Liv's intentions may have been, she stressed I was to be a donor only. Nothing more. I can't get emotionally involved."

"I don't know what to do. Maddie said Liv had been adamant about caring for the babies on her own, so she sent her home. Aside from some brief text messages over the last two weeks, I haven't really spoken to her. Based on the little information I have, Liv may be suffering from postpartum depression."

"Oh man." Wes shoved his hands in his pockets. "That's pretty serious."

"I don't think she'd harm herself, but Liv doesn't do well with failure." They'd grown up with failure in every way imaginable and they both worked hard to avoid it now. "I'm wondering if she recognized what was happening to her and removed herself from the girls to protect them. Possibly to get help."

"Would she have had that much clarity?"

"She called Maddie and asked her to come over and babysit. And then there was the note she left telling Maddie to call me. When I checked her room, her luggage was missing. Her closet and quite a few drawers were partially empty leading me to assume she packed for a trip of some sort. She planned every step. It's not erratic behavior. She's either on a long vacation or she checked herself in somewhere."

"What did the note say?" Jade withdrew the folded slip of paper from her bag and handed it to him. He read it, then turned it over as if expecting to find more. "This is all she wrote?"

Jade nodded. "That's it."

Wes scrubbed the day-old scruff on his chin. "This sounds permanent. I'll talk to Harlan and see what he can find out."

"Your brother? Why? What can he do?"

"He's a deputy sheriff."

"Then keep him out of it." Jade snatched the note back from him, suddenly wishing she hadn't come to see Wes. "The police and social workers always believe they're doing what's best for the children when they don't see or understand the whole picture. I'll handle this."

He stared at her as if she had two heads. "Look, I don't like the idea of involving my brother, either, but you can't do it alone. Triplets are hard enough for a conventional family, let alone a single parent. Your sister's a prime example of that. Do you have help at the house?"

"Maddie said she'd be willing to stay for however long I need her."

"Unless Maddie quit her job since I left in January, she works full-time."

"Are you offering your help?"

"As in physically be there with you?" Wes held up his hands and stepped back. "Oh no. I don't want to see them and please don't force them on me."

"I would never force a child on anyone. They deserve better than that. I only came here because I thought you might have an idea where she went. My mistake."

Jade trudged back to her car, almost twisting her ankle in the process. What the hell had possessed her to wear high heels to a ranch? Stupidity along with vanity. She'd wanted to show Wes that despite the horrible rumors he'd spread about her in school, she had made something of herself. Eleven years later and she was still letting his opinion matter.

FOR A SMALL TOWN, the drive back to Liv's house felt like an eternity. Except for a handful of neighbors, her sister lived fairly isolated on the outskirts of Saddle Ridge. Maddie greeted her at the door, tense in anticipation of good news.

"How are the girls?"

"Still asleep. I expect them up soon. Once one's awake, the rest follow. Did you hear anything?"

"No." Jade slipped off her shoes and kicked them aside. "I ran into a friend of hers, though. Wes Slade."

"He must be home for the wedding and christenings."

"You know about them?"

"They only invited the entire town."

Of course, they had. There was nothing like living in a small town. "So, they were good friends?"

"Until he moved to Texas. His leaving really upset Liv since he hadn't even bothered to say goodbye. He's a hottie and a half, but the two of them never hooked up. Probably because he was hooking up with everyone else in the county." Maddie's face turned pink. "Present company excluded."

Jade was all too familiar with Wes's libido.

"My sister never mentioned him. When did they become friends?"

"I'm not really sure since I didn't live here then, but based on different things she's said, I've always assumed it was around the time Wes's father was killed."

"I remember Liv mentioning that, but I didn't realize they knew each other that well." Jade had never discussed Wes or the rumors he had started. The rumors that led to one of his friends assaulting her. Liv had had enough going on between school and working whenever she could to save for college. Regardless, Liv had to have heard the rumors from her friends. Saddle Ridge was too small of a town not to. Was that why she kept her friendship with Wes from her? Or had Wes said something?

"I tried calling Liv again, and it went straight to voice mail. I left a message telling her you were here and that the girls were fine."

"Nothing about them missing her?" Jade asked.

"I—I don't remember exactly what I said. Should I have?"

Jade dropped her bag on the antique hall table in the foyer. "If she's suffering from some form of postpartum depression I'd like to believe hearing the children miss her would prove how much they need her. That's just speculation on my part." She wondered if her sister would interpret their being fine as confirmation she'd done the right thing. But Maddie blamed herself enough already. Jade didn't need to add to it. "Why don't you head home, take a shower and relax for the night. I appreciate you going above and beyond like you have."

"Are you sure?" Maddie gnawed on her bottom lip. "I realize you were here when the girls were born, but do you know how to take care of an infant? Let alone three?"

"I'm sure I can handle feeding them, changing a few diapers and putting them to bed." Jade's hands flew to her chest. "Oh my God! Liv was breast-feeding."

Maddie shook her head. "No, it didn't work out. She wasn't producing enough milk and was unbelievably sore. They started on formula pretty early."

Jade had headed back to LA eight days after the girls were released from the hospital. "She never told me."

"She probably wouldn't have told me if I hadn't been staying here. It really upset her."

"I bet." Jade imagined her sister thought not being able to breast-feed as the ultimate failure.

"Have you ever mixed formula before?"

"Can't say that I have." Jade sighed.

"Come on." Maddie motioned for her to follow. "There's kind of a formula to making formula and it all starts with boiling water."

By the time Maddie walked her through the steps, Jade understood why women opted to breast-feed. Even though the can came with directions, she took detailed notes, not wanting to risk a mistake.

"Just remember to toss out any mixed formula after twenty-four hours. You can make a large batch of it, but it's not like milk. You can't keep a gallon in the fridge for a week. If any of them don't finish their bottle, toss it because their saliva can contaminate the formula."

"Got it. I'm assuming this is the bottle sterilizer?" Jade pointed to a large dome-shaped appliance sitting on the counter.

"Yes. You can also run their pacifiers through there. But—" Maddie opened the cabinet next to the sink and removed three bottomless bottles and a box "—it's more convenient to use these with the liners. That way the nipples are the only thing you'll need to clean. Just toss the liners in the trash."

After a crash course in infant feeding, Maddie left for the night. Jade peeked in at the girls before heading to the guest room to change. She stood in the doorway as she'd done earlier, almost afraid to get any closer to the children who were biologically hers. She still had a tough time wrapping her brain around it. If she intended to take care of them until Liv returned, she needed to remember Liv was their real mother, not her.

She tiptoed across the room to their cribs, choking back tears. They were beautiful, and she'd help create them. The inexplicable desire to hold them overwhelmed her. She wanted to tell them how much she loved them and that she'd never abandon them. How bad had things gotten for her sister to walk away from her children?

She reached over the side of the crib and lightly ran her hand over one of their matching white-and-pink cotton bunny onesies. *Matching!* How would she tell the girls apart? They were fraternal triplets, but they looked alike to her. Especially at this age. Liv and Maddie could tell them apart, but Jade hadn't spent enough time around them yet. If it wasn't for the large *A*, *H* and *M* stenciled on the wall above their respective cribs she wouldn't have known who was Audra, Hadley or Mackenzie.

"What if I mix them up?"

Hadley stirred at the sound of her voice but didn't wake up. Jade scanned the room. She needed something to distinguish them from each other. Nail polish came to mind, but she feared they'd chew it off. She ran back downstairs to Liv's office and dug a black permanent marker out of the drawer. She'd have to write their first initial on the sole of their foot until she researched a better solution online. Maybe the pediatrician could offer a suggestion. She had to call there anyway to find out when the babies' next appointment was. First, she had to fabricate a plausible excuse as to why she was calling and not her sister. She didn't want to arouse suspicion about Liv.

One triplet began to cry as she reached the top step. She ran into the room, pulled off the marker cap with her teeth and wrote a large *H* on the bottom of Hadley's foot when the odor of a full diaper smacked her square in the jaw.

"Good heavens. For a tiny little thing, that is one big stink." Jade lifted Hadley into her arms as Audra began crying. Within seconds, the room was full of shrieks and smelly diapers. She couldn't pacify or change the girls fast enough. She wasn't even sure how to get them downstairs to feed them. Maddie would. Jade went to pull her phone from her pocket before remembering she left it in her bag. "Okay, I guess we're going down one at a time."

Mackenzie started crying louder than the other two before she reached the hallway. "What is it, sweetheart?" She cradled her against her chest, afraid to put her down. "You have a clean diaper and I will feed you in a few minutes." Mackenzie's tear streaked face turned red while her tiny arms flailed in the air. Jade adjusted the baby's position and sat in the rocking chair. "Shh, I've got you. I know you miss your mommy, but I'm here."

Mackenzie's cries continued along with her two sisters and Jade wondered if Liv had postpartum depression or if she'd needed a sanity break. She easily saw how this could try even a saint's patience after a while. Jade couldn't do this alone. She needed help.

WES SAT IN LIV'S driveway for ten minutes before he got the nerve to walk up the porch stairs and knock on the door. Once he did, he heard a baby cry from inside. He hadn't even considered he might wake them up. He hadn't considered much on the drive over except that he hadn't given Jade his phone number and he didn't have hers. His concern for Liv was worth the risk of seeing the girls.

Wes's heart pounded in his chest as a cold sweat formed across his brow. His biological daughters were inside that house. It was the closest he'd ever been to them and all he wanted to do was run. Why hadn't he called Liv's house and left a message on the answering machine if Jade didn't answer? Because he hadn't thought this through. The reality he'd created three children with the bully responsible for the beatings he'd received in the high school locker room struck him harder than a runaway Mack truck.

"Maddie, I need you!"

A chill ran down Wes's spine at the sound of Jade's desperate plea. He grabbed the knob and flung the door open, causing it to bang against the interior wall. "Jade!" He ran toward the baby cries, uncertain what he might find. He stuck his head in the numerous rooms that branched off the center hall of the old farmhouse. "Jade, where are you?" he asked as he reached the kitchen, only to find Jade, barefoot and disheveled holding one screaming infant in her arms while the other two wailed from bouncy chairs perched on top of the table.

His heart stopped beating at the sight of them. His

daughters. His. They had his DNA, his genes, his—
Wes grabbed the doorjamb.

"Thank God you're here." She took a step toward him.

He shook his head, trying not to break eye contact
with her for fear he'd look into the eyes of one of his
daughters. "Why are they crying?"

"Wes, meet Audra." She held the infant out to him.
"Please help me."

His arms rose automatically to take her without
hesitation as his body betrayed his will. He closed his
eyes, not wanting to see the life he'd helped create. The
weight of Audra in his arms made her all that more real.
Her cries stopped as a soft mew emanated from the tiny
bundle. He didn't want to look. But he couldn't not look.
He needed to see his daughter.

"Oh my God." His heart sprang back to life.

"What is it?" Jade frantically asked.

"She's beautiful," he whispered.

"They all are. We made quite the heartbreakers."

He lifted his gaze to hers. The edginess had faded
to a gentle softness. Even with her stained blouse and
what appeared to be a black marker streak across her
left cheek, she exuded beauty. "I guess we did." He lowered his eyes to the other two girls contentedly sucking
on the bottles Jade held for them. And then he saw more
black marker. "Did you write on their feet?"

"I had to. I couldn't tell them apart. They're not identical, but they sure look that way to me."

Wes cautiously stepped forward as if walking on ice.
He'd held a baby before. He'd been around plenty of

children in his twenty-nine years. Somehow, these three seemed more fragile than any of the others combined.

"The nose on that one is a little more upturned." Wes glanced at the infant's foot. "What does the *M* stand for?"

"Liv never told you their names?"

"She sent me a birth announcement, or what I assumed was one. I never opened it."

"Wow, you really haven't spoken to her in months because she chose those names in January."

"I stopped taking her calls when she told me she was having triplets." He reached for the third bottle sitting on the table and held it up. "May I?"

"Be my guest. She refused to eat for me."

Wes sat in the chair across from her and held the bottle to Audra's tiny lips. She hesitated for a second before eagerly drawing on the nipple. Her eyes reminded him of Jade's…big, blue and the color of the Montana sky on a bright summer day. He wished somebody would pinch him because feeding his daughter was the most surreal experience of his life.

"I hate that I didn't call. It bothered me then, but it bothers me more now. I can't help wondering if my abandonment contributed to her leaving."

"I won't criticize you for walking away because if Liv and I weren't sisters, I may have done the same thing."

Jade's candor surprised him. "So, you still haven't told me what the *M* stands for."

"Mackenzie and the other is Hadley."

"Audra, Mackenzie and Hadley." His cheeks hurt from smiling. "It's a pleasure to meet you. I'm—" He wasn't sure how to introduce himself.

"You're a friend of their mother. That's all we can ever be."

Ten minutes ago, Wes didn't even want to be a friend to anyone connected to the children, now it hardly seemed enough.

"How is this supposed to work? You can't even feed the three of them on your own."

"That's not fair." Jade held a bottle up to the light to see how much formula remained in the liner. "This was my first try. Although I'm not sure what my sister was thinking when she told Maddie to call me. I'm not exactly mother material. My job's super demanding and consumes most of my time."

"What do you do?"

"I own a high-end event management company in Los Angeles. You could say I'm a party planner to the stars. I'm surprised my sister didn't tell you."

He would never have guessed she'd chosen that career path. He figured she would have chosen… Wes stared at her, not recognizing the woman she was today. He'd never given much thought to what she did after high school. Once she'd moved away, he had been thrilled to have her out of his life. Even though her cruelty still stuck with him.

"Your sister rarely mentioned you."

Jade recoiled at his comment. "Well, that's nice. At least you didn't tell her how much you hated me."

Just as much as you hated me. "I met your sister the day of my father's funeral. We were both at the Iron Horse, saddled up to the bar. She recognized me and offered her condolences. At the time, I was too lost in my grief to realize who she was. That was the night she and her husband called it quits. She was hurting and I couldn't see past my anger over my father's death."

"I'm so sorry you had to go through that, but I'm glad you two found comfort in each other."

Wes nodded. "That old saying about misery loving company is true. We were two lonely souls drowning our sorrows. The next day I didn't even remember her name, but we kept meeting there night after night and as time went on, we met less at the bar and more in a booth with coffee and a bite to eat. It was only then I realized she was your sister. I couldn't have gotten through those days without her."

"I tried talking her into moving out to LA when Kevin left. She refused to leave this place. We'd bounced around so much in foster care that once she had this house, hell would freeze over before she left it."

"She didn't really discuss where you two had lived while growing up, but I got a real sense that home meant everything to her." Liv had sidestepped most references to her childhood, and he'd assumed she'd wanted to keep that door closed forever. He understood where she'd been coming from and never pressed further. "Our friendship started out consoling each other over what we'd lost. My father and her husband. Once we got that out of our systems, our conversations shifted to the future and what we wanted out of life. She talked a lot about wanting a family of her own."

"Liv's not one to dwell in the past." Jade sat both bottles on the table and lifted Mackenzie into her arms.

"No, she's not." Wes waited for Jade to grab a burp towel, but she didn't. "You need to hold her a little more upright and against your shoulder. And you should have something to protect your shirt because she will spit up." He stood, still cradling Audra in one arm while he opened and closed drawers until he found what he was looking for. He draped a towel over Jade's shoulder, noticing the softness of her hair against his hand as he did so. "Watch me." Audra had finished her bottle. He set it on the counter and shifted her in his arms. "Hold her like this and lightly pat her back."

"How did you get so good at this?" Jade mirrored him.

"I've had practice. More than a man who never wants kids should." Wes had seen enough dysfunction in his own family to kill any desire he'd ever had of settling down. His father's death had fractured the final fragments that had held the Slades together. Getting tossed off a bull hurt a lot less than losing someone you love. Three of his four siblings had maintained a close relationship to each other, but their mom had taken off for sunny California. Much like Jade had. Nevertheless, he'd learned to keep an emotional distance ever since. "Any more thoughts where your sister might be?"

"Tomorrow I'll call every postpartum depression treatment center I can find, including over the border in Canada just to be on the safe side. She's an adult, so I'm not sure if anyone can legally tell me if she's there, but I at least have to try."

"Well, the reason I came here tonight was to give you my phone number and to get yours."

"You could've called the house and given it to me seeing as you didn't want to meet the girls."

"That dawned on me while I was knocking on the front door." Wes sniffed the top of Audra's head. She smelled like new car smell for humans. "From the looks and sounds of things, it's a good thing I did. Where's Maddie?"

"I sent her home. She'd been here for over twenty-four hours. The woman hadn't even had a shower or change of clothes."

"It looks like you could use the same."

"Thanks a lot." Jade attempted to smooth the front of her shirt.

Wes laughed as he settled Audra into the empty bouncy seat and lifted Hadley into his arms. "I didn't mean that to sound as insulting as it did. It was a poorly worded offer to watch the girls while you take a few moments for yourself."

"Are you sure?"

"Considering I made a commitment to help bring these three into the world, I think I can commit to baby-sitting while you shower."

"Thank you."

"But…this is a onetime deal, Jade." He didn't want to delude her into thinking he'd changed his mind about being involved in their lives. "I'm here now, but once I walk out that door, I'm not coming back."

He couldn't—wouldn't—risk his heart. It was already on the verge of shattering into a thousand pieces.

Chapter Three

Jade awoke with the worst backache of her life. She eased her body out of the rocking chair she had tried to sleep in last night. Staying in the guest bedroom down the hall proved futile after hours of tossing and turning. It didn't help that she kept getting up and checking on the girls every few minutes. The video baby monitor was great during the day, but it was difficult to see at night when the only light in the room was an elephant lamp on the dresser against the far wall.

How had her sister done it alone in a house this size? It was the middle of summer and the place creaked whenever the wind blew. She could only imagine how loud it was during the blustery Montana winter. There was too much house, too much baby and not enough time to breathe.

Liv had surprised Jade when she'd first mentioned in vitro. It had been one thing to want a baby with her husband, but as a single parent? Their mom had failed at single parenting ten times over. And she couldn't help wondering if their mother was part of the problem. She had never bonded with them and vice versa.

Jade tried to remember the days after the girls were born. Liv had stayed in the hospital for three days and the girls had been in the neonatal intensive care unit for almost two weeks. It had been so hectic that she hadn't noticed if Liv had bonded with the girls. Could she have missed the signs? Even though she'd been sore, Liv had been determined to get up and move around when she needed to. In hindsight, Jade shouldn't have left so soon. Work had beckoned and despite her connection to the girls, she should have sucked it up and stayed an extra couple of weeks with her sister.

Jade quietly slipped out of the nursery and grabbed her phone off the charger in the guest room. It was a few minutes after five in the morning. Los Angeles was an hour behind them, but knowing Tomás, her assistant was probably awake. The man had been her shadow for the last five years. His attention to the finest of details and endless amount of energy kept her business running smoothly. He was the only person she would ever trust to handle any given situation the way she would.

The hardwood floors groaned as she made her way to the narrow staircase leading to the kitchen. She hesitated on the top step and listened for any sign that she'd woken the girls. Confident they were still asleep, she continued downstairs and beelined for the coffeemaker. Once the caffeine began coursing through her veins, she dialed her assistant.

"Good morning, gorgeous." Tomás's chipper voice boomed through the phone. "And how is our temporary *mummy* holding up this morning?"

"Let's just say I made it through the night in one

piece." For the next fifteen minutes, she sipped coffee and filled Tomás in on yesterday's events, including Wes. Tomás had been the one person she had completely confided in about her past. He knew the good, the bad and the ugly.

"Oh, darling. You've been holding out on me." He lowered his voice to a whisper so not to wake his husband. "I just pulled up your cowboy online, and that's the finest male specimen I've seen in forever. He just oozes testosterone and ruggedness."

"Tomás!" Jade nearly knocked over her mug. "Do I need to remind you what he did to me?"

"No, but I think I need to remind you he was only a teenager back then. Now..." Tomás clucked his tongue. "He's a hundred percent man."

"I don't care when it was. Cowboys never did it for me."

"Your cowboy is a champion bull rider and his earnings last year were almost four times more than what I made."

Jade straightened in her chair. "You can see how much he made?"

"I sure can." He gave her the web address and she pulled up his stats.

"I had no idea bull riders made so much money." Jade continued to scan the page. Turned out Wes was one of the top bull riders in the country and fifth in the standings this year.

"It also seems your boy is active in social media. That's quite a good morning."

"What are you talking about? How did you find that out?"

"I went to his website, westonslade.com."

Website? "I didn't realize he was that popular."

"I thought you said you looked him up online."

"I did. But I used one of those people directories, so it showed me his place of employment first. And that's where I stopped."

She typed in the address. Okay, the website was impressive. Professionally done and sexy, yet unreservedly masculine. She clicked on the first social media account and wondered if he had a team posting for him as she did. Nope. A selfie of him lying in bed with the caption Good Morning had posted a few minutes earlier and it already had close to a thousand likes. The hair on the back of her neck rose as she read one erotic reply after another. Most from women although there were a handful of men on there too.

"I swear, Tomás," she warned. "I better not see your name pop up."

Tomás cleared his throat and the sound of him rapidly hitting a key on his computer reverberated through the phone.

"I can't believe you."

"It's not like I hit Send."

She continued to read the posts and noticed Wes hadn't responded to any of the comments. "Okay, so maybe he's just a narcissist."

"If I didn't know any better, I'd say your kitten claws have come out."

A flicker of movement on the baby monitor caught her attention. Hadley's legs were beginning to kick.

Judging by last night's diaper changes, that was the sign another was coming.

"I'll have to call you back. The little ones are waking up."

"Okay, love. You take care of those beauties and I'll touch base with you sometime this afternoon."

An hour later, Jade was either on the verge of tears or a nervous breakdown. She couldn't do this full-time. And she was used to dealing with difficult. But Hollywood bridezillas were easier to handle. And potty trained.

When Maddie stopped by around six thirty, Jade almost threw herself at her feet and begged for mercy.

"Oh, Jade." Maddie's eyes trailed up and down the length of her. "What have they done to you?"

Jade thrust Mackenzie into her arms. "How can anyone in their right mind think having a baby is a good idea?"

Maddie laughed. "You must've had some night if you're swearing off kids altogether."

"I've never wanted children. Never. I'm too busy and too active to be tied down. And so was my sister up until she decided to do this. She and Kevin were always off backpacking or flying to Europe for the weekend. It was constantly go, go, go. And even after they split up, she would tell me about the spontaneous weekend trips she would take to Texas or Wyoming or— I'll be damned."

"What?"

"She was following Wes on the road, wasn't she?" Jade couldn't for the life of her figure out why her sister hadn't mentioned his name or at the very least, that she was going to rodeos.

"I wouldn't say she was following him. She met up with him if his competitions fell on the weekend."

"And there wasn't anything between them?"

"No. I can honestly say I don't believe they ever even kissed."

She didn't think Wes was capable of having a platonic relationship with a woman. She thought she knew her sister better than anyone did. She couldn't have been more wrong. It didn't make sense.

"I take it you haven't heard from Liv?"

"No." Maddie smiled down at Mackenzie in her arms. "I wanted to call, but I don't want to drive her further away."

Jade had fought the same urge throughout the night. "I didn't, either. Once the kids fell asleep, I called a bunch of treatment centers specializing in postpartum depression. They were all in-patient facilities within a day's drive from here."

"And nothing?"

"It was an exercise in futility. No matter how much I pleaded, privacy laws prevented them from releasing any information. I left the same message for Liv at each place in case she's there, 'Just let us know you're safe.' I'll call out-patient facilities today and do the same thing. Other than that, I'm at a loss. This can't go on indefinitely." Jade hated to involve the police, but the more time passed, the more concerned she became. She honestly thought Liv would have reached out by now. "One day, okay, I get it. There's a lot of stress involved with caring for triplets. But we're going on two days and postpartum depression or not, a text message would have been nice."

"What happens if she doesn't come back? Can you legally take them with you to California?"

"I'm not sure." The same scenario had played through Jade's head earlier. "If I just leave with them and she returns in a frazzled state, she could accuse me of kidnapping."

"You don't think she'd do that, do you?"

"Yesterday, I didn't. Today, I'm realizing there's a lot I didn't know about my sister. Before I can leave with them, I would have to report Liv missing and the kids would go in the system. They'll probably have to evaluate me and my home in LA before releasing them to me. I'm Liv's only relative so I hope that counts for something, but I can't be a hundred percent certain the girls won't go in foster care. I need to contact an attorney."

"I can put together some names, if you'd like." Maddie eased Mackenzie into her bouncy chair.

"Thanks, but I'll call the one Liv used to set up the donor paperwork."

"You know who she used?"

"Ah." Jade froze. Her brain short-circuited as she tried to cover her slip. Liv had wanted everyone to believe she used two anonymous donors. "She mentioned someone a few times. I'm assuming she has the name and number in her office. I'm sure I'll recognize it when I see it."

Maddie nodded, seemingly unconcerned. "Before I forget, today's garbage day. Monday, as well."

"That was on my list of questions to ask you." She'd made many lists in between phone calls, ranging from to-dos to how-tos. There was satisfaction in checking off a task as she went about her day. "Would you mind watching the girls for a few minutes while I get it together?"

"Sure, I don't have to be to work until nine o'clock so I have time. Take a shower and get yourself cleaned up, including whatever that black mark is on your cheek."

"Black mark?" Jade walked into the small half bath off the kitchen and flipped on the light. "Are you kidding me?" She had a three-inch-long black permanent marker streak starting at the corner of her mouth going toward her ear. "I can't believe he didn't tell me."

Jade had taken such a quick shower last night while Wes had watched the girls, she hadn't bothered to look in the mirror.

"He was here for quite a while." Maddie's voice lilted with implication.

Jade rolled her eyes. Maddie must have seen his truck in the driveway. "We were just comparing notes, and he watched the kids long enough for me to shower and change."

"Apparently it wasn't long enough. You have some time, go do what you have to do."

Jade ran upstairs and grabbed the bathroom garbage along with the bag from the Diaper Genie.

"I never thought to ask what you do for a living," Jade said as she returned to the kitchen and lifted the lid off the trash can alongside the counter.

"I'm a court reporter. It's nowhere near as glamorous as your job. I can only imagine what it's like meeting all those celebrities."

Jade inwardly laughed. Her job was far from glamorous. "I don't just have celebrity clients, but they are the majority of my business. And let me tell you, those happy smiles you see plastered on the pages of magazines aren't always real. Underneath they have the same fears and concerns as the rest of us. Sometimes I feel sorry for them. Every move they make, especially when it comes to their wedding, gets photographed and scrutinized. I can't even begin to tell you the lengths we have to go to sometimes just to get a client to a venue. It can be a logistical nightmare. Some days seem like they'll never end, but I wouldn't trade it in for the world."

How was she going to run a business and care for Mackenzie, Hadley and Audra? She never wanted kids and now she had three. No. She squared her shoulders and tied the garbage bag closed. She had to stay positive. Liv would come back and everything would be fine. Jade opened the back door off the mudroom and almost tripped over three car seats sitting on the top step.

"Okay, we need to find a better place for these."

"Oh my God!" Maddie jumped up. "Those are from Liv's car. When did she put them there?"

"I have no idea." Jade moved one aside and ran down the steps into the yard, hoping to find her sister.

"They are a little damp from the morning dew," Maddie said. "They've been out here for a while."

Jade wanted to collapse in the grass and cry. *Where are you, Liv?* She took a deep breath and plodded back up the stairs to the mudroom. "I don't think I opened this door yesterday. Did you?"

"I did when I put the garbage in the can. That was sometime in the early afternoon. It had to have been after that."

"Then she came back." Jade's heart rose to her throat. "But when?"

Jade closed her eyes and hoped it wasn't when she and Wes had fed the girls in the kitchen last night. Liv would have had a clear view of them from the steps. Seeing the biological parents together with their children was the last thing her sister needed. She just prayed it hadn't pushed Liv further over the edge.

WES HAD THOUGHT the worst mistake of his life had been the day he miscalculated Crazy Town's spin direction and damn near died when the bull tossed and trampled him. He'd changed his mind when Liv told him the embryo transfer had been a success. It still hadn't compared to the mistake he made last night.

There had been an uncontrollable force driving him to Liv's house. He'd gone and done the one thing he'd sworn he never would. And now that he'd met his daughters, he couldn't get their tiny cherub faces out of his head. His heart couldn't handle seeing them again knowing they weren't his to keep. Not that he wanted to keep them. Just the opposite. The sooner he got out of town, the better.

He'd spent most of the night down at the stables to avoid Garrett's countless questions about Jade and her emergency. He wished Jade had just called and left a message instead of talking to his brother. Then again, if she hadn't stalked him at the ranch, he never would have spoken with her and she knew it.

His phone rang, and he was almost afraid to check the display. It was half past nine and it could be anyone, from his management team to one of his friends. But his gut told him it was Jade. The thought alone both frightened and excited him.

He braved a glance at the screen. Her name flashed at him like a rodeo clown waving a red flag. He froze long enough for the call to go to voice mail. He couldn't talk to her. Talking would lead to seeing his daughters again. His daughters. They were no longer a concept. Even after their due date had passed, Wes had refused to think of them as tiny humans almost two thousand miles away from his new home in Ramblewood, Texas. Now he had no choice.

He had held them in his arms and they had imprinted themselves on his heart. How could he walk away and go back to life as usual? Especially when they were growing up in his hometown where every time he visited his brothers and their growing families he ran the risk of running into them. And what would happen when they got older and started driving or playing sports? He was bound to see their names in the newspaper or mentioned by a neighbor or friend. Saddle Ridge was a small town and nothing escaped anyone.

Wes stormed to the tack room. He needed to go for a ride and clear his head. The voice mail notification chimed from his back pocket. As much as he wanted to ignore it, he couldn't. His finger hovered over the play button, praying Jade had called to say she had found Liv and everything was fine.

"Wes, it's Jade. I know you have your phone in your hand because you posted a pic online less than five minutes ago. At least it was better than the tacky one of you in bed. Anyway, I'm calling to tell you Liv came back to the house sometime yesterday or during the night. I don't know when or how long she stayed, but it may have been when you were here. Please call me as soon as you get this. I'm scared of how she may have reacted if she saw us together with the girls."

WES TOOK THE front porch steps of Liv's house two at a time. Jade opened the door and pulled him inside before he had a chance to knock. He told himself repeatedly on the drive over he was there only for Liv's well-being. Any attachment to the girls was off-limits.

"Thank you for coming. I know this is the last place you want to be."

Wes followed her into the small living room off the main hallway. He'd half expected to see Audra, Hadley and McKenzie when he turned the corner, instead the room looked exactly as it always had.

"It doesn't even look like a baby, let alone three babies, lives here."

"Exactly." Jade paced the length of the small off-white area rug. "We were so busy feeding the girls yesterday I didn't get a chance to show you this." She grabbed his hand and led him down the hall to a narrow closet. The gesture was innocent enough, but her palm against his felt more intimate than a kiss. Within seconds she released him, and damned if he didn't miss her touch already. He balled his fist, refusing to feel anything for the woman. "This is what I mean when I say Liv knew what she was doing."

She swung the closet open and flipped on the overhead light. There were numerous neatly stacked, transparent lidded bins with index cards taped to the front of them listing each one's contents. Baby toys, baby blankets, baby photo albums…all generically labeled.

"Why is everything in the closet?"

"These had all been in various rooms when I left a little over a month ago. Sometime between now and then, she ordered storage containers and packed everything away."

Wes wandered around the first floor of the house, peering into each room. "I've never been upstairs, but nothing down here looks any different from before she got pregnant. The place was always spotless. Is it possible she took the bins out when she needed them?"

Jade shook her head. "It doesn't make sense. Those photo albums used to be on the coffee table. She couldn't wait to fill them. I looked inside and there are three, possibly four pages' worth of photos. And the baby blankets…she was so proud that she'd learned how to crochet for her daughters. Those are shoved in a box too."

"What about the nursery? Did she change anything in there?"

"No." Jade started up the stairs, but Wes's feet refused to follow. "Are you coming?"

"Aren't the girls up there?"

Her shoulders sagged at the question. "So that's it? Last night was a onetime deal and you're never going to see them again."

"I thought I already made that clear." What part of not wanting to be a parent didn't she understand? He had to set boundaries before she expected more from him. "I'm not here for them. I'm here because you said Liv came back to the house and you're afraid she saw us together. I'm here because I'm worried about her. I'm not worried about the girls. I trust you with them."

"How very big of you." She closed the distance between them, her eyes blazing with anger and fear. "Hell, I'm surprised you haven't snapped a picture of them and posted it all over the internet to see how many likes and follows you can get."

Wes put a hand on her arm. "I know you're upset, and I meant what I said yesterday. I'll do whatever I can to help you find Liv. But please, don't take it out on me. This isn't my fault just like it isn't your fault."

Jade dropped her gaze. "It is our fault. We missed the signs. You taking off to Texas is no different from me flying back to LA as fast as I could. We both abandoned her."

"We were only donors." Wes bit back the bile he now associated with the word. "Those kids aren't ours. And you didn't abandon Liv. You were there when the babies were born. You helped bring them home. You're caring for them night and day. You're living in the same house with them. They're the first thing you see in the morning and they're the last thing you see at night. I don't even have to be here to recognize you're getting attached to them."

"Of course I am." Tears filled her eyes. "I never wanted to feel this way, but they're our daughters. How can you not get attached?"

"They are your nieces, but they can't ever be anything to me. That's how Liv wanted it."

Jade tried to pull from his grip, but he refused to let go. Not when she was in so much pain. Her heart beat wildly against him as he held her tight to his chest. Despite the past or the resentment he still felt toward her, he wanted nothing more than to ease the guilt she carried.

"It's okay." He smoothed her hair and rested his cheek against the top of her head. "It's going to be okay. We'll find Liv, make sure she gets the help she needs and bring her home to her children."

"I'm scared she's not going to be okay or that she'll do this again." Jade sobbed against him. "She came back, Wes. She was here, and she left. She walked away twice. How could she do that?"

Wes eased her onto the couch, summoning every ounce of strength he had not to panic. Between the abandoned triplets he'd never wanted to be involved with and Liv's fragile emotional state, he felt the overwhelming need to protect the Scott women, even if that included Jade…the woman who had made his life pure hell.

"Tell me what happened."

After Jade explained about the car seats she'd found earlier, he figured there was a fifty-fifty chance Liv had seen them together. Since she'd purposely kept their identities from the other, he understood how watching him and Jade with the girls might upset her.

"I'm not trying to belittle your concerns in any way, but why do you think seeing us together would push her over the edge?"

Jade shifted on the couch to face him and tucked her bare legs underneath her jean-short-covered bottom. Coupled with her deep V-neck white cotton T-shirt, she wore ultracasual extremely well. A little too well since his jeans felt snugger than they had a minute ago.

"I think my sister had a thing for you and maybe still does."

Wes threw his head back and laughed, knocking his hat on the back of the couch. He removed it and set it brim side up on the coffee table while running his other hand through his hair.

"Trust me, your sister was not interested in me romantically."

"How can you be so sure?"

"Because she's still in love with Kevin. That's one broken heart I don't think she'll ever get past."

"She divorced him years ago."

"He divorced her," Wes corrected, surprised she didn't know. "I was with her the night she was served. And she was served very publicly in the middle of the Iron Horse."

Jade's mouth hung open in disbelief. "Is she so afraid of failure that she has to hide her pain from me? Or am I that cold of a person she didn't think I would understand?"

Wes couldn't believe the words coming out of her mouth. "Get over yourself. It isn't about you. From the little she told me about both of your pasts, she was the one taking care of you while you did whatever you wanted."

"That was hardly the case."

"Really, because the Jade I remember was constantly getting into trouble. You were an angry kid. And mean. God, you were mean."

"I'll own up to having an attitude, but I was mean to only you and that's because you said I'd slept with you. Your lie almost got me raped by your friend."

"What?" His fists clenched. Wes couldn't imagine any of his friends forcing themselves on a girl. "Who are you talking about?"

"Oh, come on. You know damn well I'm talking about your buddy Burke. Every time I saw you two together afterward you were laughing at me."

"Burke tried to rape you?" A slow rage began to build in his chest. Burke had been more of a rival than a friend. They'd competed against each other in all aspects of their lives. From bull riding to girls. "When?"

"Our ninth-grade fall harvest dance. How can you not remember?" Jade jumped up from the couch as if it was on fire and faced him. "You two were sitting on the gym bleachers laughing and pointing at me. I'd had enough and decided to leave. Burke followed me into the hallway, threw me against the lockers and reached under my skirt. He tore off my underwear!" Her eyes filled with tears. "He told me he wanted what I gave you. I physically had to fight him to break free. He had his zipper down and was ready to go."

Wes's stomach churned. "He said you two had hooked up. He even showed me your underwear. I was crushed you chose him over me. Jade, I had no idea what really happened."

"It wasn't consensual! Torn underwear should have been your clue?" Jade shook her head in disgust. "It happened because you told everyone we had slept together. You told everyone I was easy. He assumed I was shareable when you and I had only kissed."

"Yeah and we had dated for almost a month." The words came out of his mouth before he could stop them.

"So that meant I owed you sex?" Jade's face reddened. "We started dating, like, my second week of ninth grade. Liv and I had just come out of another group home and had moved in with a new foster family. I hadn't even told my sister about you. I was trying to learn everyone's name and get acclimated to a new town. I was fourteen years old and you kept pushing me to go further than I was ready. And then you broke up with me because I wouldn't. Do you have any idea how that made me feel?"

"I'm sorry," Wes whispered. He lifted his gaze to hers. "Everything was a competition to me back then. I was hurt that you didn't like me as much as I liked you. I didn't even know what sex was. I mean I did, but I hadn't done it yet. Burke had. So I lied and said I had too. He was the only one I told." He rose from the couch, torn between wanting to comfort her and beating the crap out of Burke. His old rival had moved to

New Mexico after high school, but the next time they crossed paths on the rodeo circuit, he'd be damn sure to teach him a lesson.

"Burke taunted me every chance he could, and you were right there next to him. We had just been placed with a really nice foster family, and Liv and I finally believed we had a place to call home. As nice as it was, it was never easy. At least not for me. I felt like I had a scarlet letter emblazoned on my chest, thanks to you. And two years later, on Christmas Eve when my foster mom's brother tried to force himself on me, I believed it was my fault, because it had happened to me once before."

"Please tell me he didn't—"

"Rape me?" Jade violently shook her head. "No. Liv walked in, saw what was happening and kicked his ass. But when the police came, they didn't care what I said. He claimed I had been the aggressor and they took his word over mine."

Wes felt sick. One of his brothers had recently dealt with a serious bullying issue involving his daughter and Wes had been so angry when he heard that, he had wanted to drive straight through from Texas to Montana to confront her attackers. He'd never considered himself one of those people. But he had been. And so had Jade. As much as he wanted to confront her about her bullying, he refused to turn his apology around on her. "I never intended to put you in physical danger or make you feel like any less of a person."

"That rumor followed me around until the day I graduated. I'm sure your brother is a great deputy sheriff, but any faith I had in the system disappeared that night. Instead of arresting my attacker, they sent me to a group home. Liv was eighteen then and she immediately petitioned the courts for guardianship. Within the month, the state had released me into her care." Jade began to pace the length of the small room. "We struggled to survive after that, but we did it. Liv worked two jobs and still managed to attend college full-time on the scholarship she'd won. I worked every day after school and on weekends to help pay the bills. I owe my sister for all she did back then, and I refuse to let her down." She stopped less than a foot in front of him and folded her arms tight across her chest. "And after what you did, I think you owe me too."

He'd call them even after what she'd done in retaliation all those years ago, but the determined set of her chin left him fearing where her next sentence would lead if he disagreed. "Fine."

"We created those three lives upstairs. And despite our donor contracts or how we feel about the situation, we have an obligation to Liv to make sure they're cared for. I can't do this alone. Outside of hiring a stranger, you're my only choice. Since you're in town, I'm asking you to help me. You can stay in one of the guest rooms."

"Whoa, you want me to move in here?" Wes may have been willing to handle the grocery shopping or running whatever errands or chores she needed done, but living under the same roof with her and the girls was out of the question. "That would send up all sorts of red flags to my family."

"I just told you I can't do this alone." She stared up

at him. "I highly doubt you want to run the risk of the girls not getting what they need or heaven forbid, getting hurt because I only have two arms? What if there's a fire? I thought about that last night. I don't know what Liv would have done in that situation."

Guilt trip launched and on target. "Fine, but kindly keep my time with them to an absolute minimum. I'll take care of the laundry, run wherever you need me to go and clean the house. Once this is over, you'll still be around the girls. I won't. There's no room for me in their lives so let's not make this any harder than it needs to be."

One of Jade's perfectly arched brows rose. "Of course."

Frustration coursed through his veins. She was handling him just like she probably handled her troublesome clients and he didn't appreciate it. He couldn't leave her to deal with this mess on her own, either. He had a week and a half until Dylan's wedding, and then it was back to Texas. This time he had no intentions of ever returning to Saddle Ridge.

Chapter Four

Jade should probably have her head examined for asking Wes to move in with her and the girls. While she'd never forgive him for the past, their talk last night had lessened her anger about the situation. She doubted she'd ever have full closure over the event that had spiraled her teen years out of control, but at least she'd discovered his intentions hadn't been as malicious as she'd thought.

Wes stayed true to his word. Since yesterday morning, he'd helped her around the house, made sure all Liv's bills and utilities were up-to-date and even washed, folded and put away countless loads of laundry. But when it came to the girls, he slept downstairs on the couch and excused himself from the room whenever they were near. Like now…he was in Liv's office researching other treatment centers and contacting some of their mutual friends while she prepared another round of formula. Now that she had mastered feeding the girls with the help of a rolled-up towel to support the bottles, she didn't need Wes at mealtime. But, despite their history, some company would've been nice.

Caring for triplets had quickly become an isolated job. He could have at least helped during diaper changes or bath time.

The house phone rang, and Jade almost broke her neck tripping over a chair when she ran to answer it.

"Hello?"

"May I please speak with Jade Scott?"

She shivered at the direct tone of the man's voice. "This is Jade."

"Ms. Scott, this is Jacob Meyer, Olivia's attorney. We met last year. Your sister asked me to contact you."

"Have you heard from Liv?" Her pulse began to beat erratically. "Is she all right?"

"Olivia asked me to call you and let you know she's safe."

"Thank heaven she's okay." Jade slumped against the counter, but her relief was short-lived. "If my sister is all right, why are you calling me? What happened?"

"Liv has checked into a recovery center and she'll be there for a minimum of thirty days, possibly longer."

Thirty days? She couldn't possibly stay in Montana for that long. "What kind of recovery center? What's wrong with her and how can I get in touch with her?"

"Contact is forbidden during the first week of treatment. She has authorized me to tell you she checked herself in for postpartum depression."

"I knew it. I should've seen the signs sooner." Jade looked up to see Wes standing in the kitchen doorway. She covered the phone with her hand. "It's Liv's attorney. He says she's in a treatment center."

"Where?" Wes asked, avoiding all eye contact with the three tiny faces fixated on him.

Jade shrugged and uncovered the phone. "Can you at least tell me where she is?"

"She asked me not to. I can tell you that I met with her yesterday and she has granted you temporary guardianship and power of attorney until she is able to return."

"Yesterday? That means she must be close. Unless she flew there. Then in that case—"

"Ms. Scott, please refrain from trying to contact your sister. Even if you called every PPD treatment center in the country, legally they are unable to acknowledge her residency. You'd be wasting your time and theirs."

"But she does plan on coming home." Wes crossed the room to her, every bit as eager for the answer as she was.

"Most definitely. Your guardianship is a temporary solution to an unfortunate situation. If it's any consolation, this isn't the first time I have had a client with PPD. They've all recovered, but the length of time in which that happens varies from person to person. Your sister's situation is more unique because of the donor aspect and the fact she's dealing with triplets. Considering the role you played in their births, I have to ask… are you prepared to be their guardian?"

Jade squeezed her eyes shut and exhaled slowly. "Without a doubt, but do those documents allow me to take them to California?"

"California? Part of your sister's recovery involves exposure therapy and a slow reintegration back into their lives. You and the children need to be available for all family sessions."

"That's further proof she's someplace relatively close."

Jacob cleared his throat. "Ms. Scott, you have to remain in Saddle Ridge. I hope you can make the necessary arrangements. Your sister's counting on you."

"I refuse to allow those children to go with anyone else." She wasn't sure how she'd make it work, but she didn't have a choice.

"I'll need you to stop by my office to go over these documents. Are you available around two this afternoon?"

"I'll be there."

Jade's body went numb as she hung up the phone. Her sister was safe, but unreachable. Now she was responsible for her biological children. Children she already felt too attached to.

"What did he say?"

"Not a lot except Liv is in an undisclosed postpartum depression—PPD as he called it—treatment facility and she'll be there for at least thirty days, if not more. He has guardianship and power of attorney papers waiting for me. Apparently, he met with Liv yesterday, so I'm assuming she came in to see him, although I guess he could have gone to wherever she is. He told me I have to stay in town so Liv can have visitation with the girls."

"That means she's close and this will be over soon." Relief swept across his face and it prickled her a bit, even though she felt the same way. They were both thinking too much about protecting themselves and not about what was best for the girls.

"I should do some shopping after the attorney's office." Jade slid onto the chair closest to Audra. She lightly squeezed the infant's chubby little toes. "I wasn't prepared to stay here for a week, let alone a month. I only packed a few things and most of Liv's prepregnancy clothes are too tight on me."

"I want to help in whatever way I can, but I can't stick around for the entire month. I have to get back to my job in Texas."

"And I have a job waiting for me in California. Correction…a business that I happen to own and June is our busiest month. Never mind all the planning that goes into each event or the millions of dollars we pay our vendors. Because you are so right, bouncing around on top of a bull for eight seconds is much more important. I don't expect anything from you past this upcoming week. And honestly, it doesn't even sound like you'll be around much anyway."

"Is this how it's going to be? Your job is more important than mine?" Wes kept his voice low. "We need to work together, not fight. I realize it's difficult to put the past aside. I also realize I need to remain a stranger in the girls' lives. Liv wanted you to be their aunt. She never wanted me to be a father beyond their creation. Once this is over, I don't plan on seeing them again. I won't be returning to Saddle Ridge."

"You're never coming back?" The thought alone sent her into a slight panic. "What about your family?"

"They are more than welcome to visit me in Texas. I have a small house down there with a guest room."

"That's it? You've already decided?"

He jammed his hands in his pockets. "I can't put myself or them through it. The more they see of me, the more questions they'll ask later."

Jade knew he was right, she'd just hated the thought of him walking away from his hometown forever. Not that she should care. But Wes had deep roots in Saddle Ridge. Something her damaged past never allowed her to have. He belonged near family. And Liv belonged near her. There was nothing tying her sister to Montana and Jade genuinely believed Liv would be happier in California. "I hate to ask you this, but since Maddie's at work, I really need you to babysit them this afternoon while I run into town. I promise not to be long."

Wes's cheeks puffed out and for a second she thought he'd give her an argument. "Do what you have to do." He strode across the kitchen and grabbed a bottle of pop from the fridge as his mini fan club watched from the table. Jade already saw little bits of him in Hadley. Especially her stubbornness. "Something's been bothering me all night. Didn't Liv have a baby shower?"

Jade nodded. "It wasn't that big though. I'm assuming you know her circle of friends. You, Maddie and Delta are the closest to her. Or at least you were until you moved away. And Delta's been battling cancer for the past few months. I don't even think she was at the shower. Liv has a few friends in town and some from her old job, but now that she works from home and her company is based out of Nebraska, she doesn't have the comradery she used to have. She made a lot of major life changes since she and Kevin divorced."

"Thanks for squeezing that subtle guilt trip in there." Wes braved a glance at the triplets, but his face showed zero emotion. How could he not smile when he looked at them? "What I was trying to get at, don't women usually receive baby swings and all sorts of big items at their showers? My sister-in-law had a huge baby registry. Aside from what you showed me in the closet, I don't see any other gifts in the house."

"I bought her the car seats and a triplet stroller along with a monthly diaper subscription. Her friends gave her gifts, but there was never a swing. Aren't they too small for them?"

"Are you kidding me?" Wes sat his drink on the counter. "I bought Belle this awesome Bluetooth infant seat that swings and rocks, mimicking the mother's movements. You can control it from your phone and adjusts in multiple positions so they can sleep, play, eat…you name it. I even gave one to Dylan's fiancée, Emma, for their new daughter. Here—" Wes tugged his phone out of the front pocket of his jeans and tapped the screen. "This is the video I took the other day of my nephew Travis—Belle and Harlan's kid—in his."

"Wow. He looks so much like the girls. Especially Mackenzie." Jade looked from the phone to the triplets who remained entranced by the man continuing to ignore them. Wes growled under his breath and Jade returned her attention to the large automated infant seat. "That looks really nice. The girls would love that. Where can I order one or three?"

Wes took the phone from her. "I got it covered." He tapped the screen again. "What's the address here? I can never remember the house number."

"You don't have to do that. They look expensive." For a man who claimed he didn't want kids, Wes certainly knew his way to an infant's heart.

"I can afford it." A hint of annoyance evident in his tone. "It's something I should have done months ago. Liv was my best friend and I never even bought her a baby gift. Regardless of my part in this, I shouldn't have shut her out the way I did."

"Seventy-five."

"Seventy-five what?"

"You asked the house number. Seventy-five Brookstone Lane."

"Oh." He entered the address into his phone. "I was expecting another guilt trip. My mistake."

"Let's just say I was silently agreeing with you and leave it at that."

"Fair enough. Unfortunately, I can't get next day air shipping since today is Friday, but they will be here on Monday."

"When do you go to South Dakota?" Not that she cared what he did. She hated to admit it, but last night she'd felt more comfortable with him there. A floor separated them and they had barely said a word to one another after he agreed to stay. Regardless, she'd worried a little less. Then again, she probably would have felt the same way if Maddie had stayed over. And since she had volunteered, maybe that was a better idea.

"Tuesday evening. I will be back sometime on Thursday. Don't forget I have two christenings tomorrow, a family celebration tomorrow night and a prewedding party on Sunday. I don't expect to be around much during the day."

"About that. I may have overreacted. You're home for such a short time and this is a special week for your family. You should be with them. Especially since you don't plan on coming back to Saddle Ridge. Maybe it is best if I hire someone."

Wes stared at her, causing her to shift uncomfortably. Sarcasm or some other retort would have been better than nothing. With Maddie around at night, she'd only need help during the day. Possibly even two people, since she needed time to work. There had to be a nanny service nearby where she could hire someone reliable and less...less Wes. She didn't want to like him, but after their talk last night and his infant seat gesture, she found herself doing just that. Although she owed him an apology of her own after what she did to him in school. "About last night—"

"I thought you didn't want a stranger around." Wes's tone bordered on accusatory.

"Only because I didn't want to explain Liv's absence. The guardianship papers make it legal and I don't have to worry what anyone else thinks. Not that I want my sister's personal problems broadcast around town." Although people might be more sympathetic to postpartum depression than Liv skipping out on her babies for a month because of a job.

"What are you going to say when someone asks where she is?"

"I don't want to lie. It makes things more complicated. I'm sure she assumed people would find out the truth. A thirty-day absence is hard to hide."

The girls finished their bottles, and she rinsed out each of the plastic liners before tossing them in the trash. She'd learned her lesson yesterday after the garbage can stunk to high heaven. The liners were more trouble than they were worth. She'd use regular bottles for their next feeding.

"I don't know how I'm supposed to feel about any of this."

Jade turned off the faucet and dried her hands before facing him. "You and me both. I think it was a mistake to involve you. I should've thought it through. Hell, I should've thought everything through." Jade prided herself on efficiently moving from one thing to another. That principle worked great in business, not so much in her personal life. "It bothers me that my sister was so emotionally distraught she had to abandon her kids in order to get help. You're telling me what you should've done for her and I'm thinking to myself how wonderful I thought I'd been by donating my eggs and enduring all the hormone injections and doctor visits. My body was bruised and my mood swings and hot flashes triggered by the hormones almost caused my entire team to quit. Never mind all the time I had to take off work."

"I had no idea it was that involved. My part was over in—well, you know." A tinge of pink creeped up his neck as he quickly reached for his drink.

"Despite my research, it had been more involved than I'd ever imagined. But she called me a hero for doing it and kept thanking me for the sacrifice." Jade lifted Hadley into her arms. "I thought I'd been this great sister by taking off even more time for the delivery, plus all the things I'd purchased for Liv and the girls. I was so busy congratulating myself, I missed the obvious. I should have been more aware of her needs and made sure she had the proper help. And I shouldn't have left so soon after the girls came home from the hospital."

"If she didn't want Maddie's help, what makes you think she would've welcomed someone else's?"

"Because Liv had talked about hiring a nanny once she went back to work, even though she was working from home. I can appreciate why she wouldn't want a nanny during those initial bonding months, but the point is I hadn't noticed a problem because I was too busy trying to escape."

Wes exhaled a slow breath and stared at Audra. She met his gaze and held the stare. And then smiled.

"Oh my God, did you see that?" Wes laughed. "She smiled. She actually smiled."

"Or she has gas. Either way, that's the first time I've seen any of them make that face. I think she likes you."

"Yeah, well." Wes cradled the back of Audra's head and scooped her into his arms. "Don't get attached to me, kid." He sat in the chair across from Jade and slowly rocked the infant. "I sympathize with your guilt. I'm sure Maddie does, too. But from what I've read on the postpartum depression websites, a lot of women try their hardest to cover up how they're really feeling because they don't want anyone to know they're not bonding with their children."

"And many times they are crying for help and nobody's listening." She had replayed every phone and video conversation over in her head last night and one thing stuck out more than anything else... Jade had purposely kept the calls short. She had made one work excuse after another to get off the phone, ignoring her sister's needs.

"You can analyze it to death, but it won't change anything. All we can do is accept what's in front of us and take it day by day. As much as I want to walk away, I can't. Whether we like it or not, we're a temporary team."

Jade hated temporary. The first sixteen years of her life had been filled with temporary. Temporary meant loss. And nine times out of ten, loss brought pain along for the ride. Even if she left tomorrow, there would be pain. As unconventional as they were, sitting around the kitchen table and holding the daughters they'd created felt natural on some alternate plane. If her heart wasn't ready to let go now, how would it ever be ready in a month?

WES HAD NEVER been more terrified in his entire life. He thought he could handle being alone in the house with Hadley, Audra and Mackenzie, but he'd underestimated their cuteness factor. Jade had tried to put them down for a nap before she left, but they were having none of it. So Wes relented to baby playtime on the mat in the center of the living room. Thank God they were too young to roll over and crawl away giving him some semblance of control. Gripping his finger was one thing. Gripping his heart was altogether different.

He checked the wall clock. Jade had only been gone for fifteen minutes. That was barely enough time to get to the attorney's office. He groaned. And she was clothes shopping afterward…he was doomed.

Mackenzie intently watched the musical, plush butterfly mobile he had set up over their play mat. Jade hadn't been kidding when she said Travis and Mackenzie looked alike. They were cousins, born days apart from one another, yet they would never know it. Wes choked down the unfamiliar lump in his throat. The startling realization that Travis and the triplets would be in the same grade, possibly even the same class all through school sucker punched him in the gut.

"How did I miss that before?" If they looked alike now, he could only imagine the resemblance as they got older. People were sure to question it. Jade had already asked Liv to move to California. Somehow he needed to convince them both that was the best thing for all of them. Then maybe he could visit his family freely again. Although in the back of his mind, he already knew he would forever associate Saddle Ridge with the three girls he would never see after this week.

Wes's eyes began to tear. "How could you do this to me?" he asked the triplets. "You weren't supposed to be cute. You weren't even supposed to let me like you. How can I not like you? Have you looked in the mirror?" Audra smiled again as if she understood. "You're adorable. I see a lot of your mom in you. I guess I shouldn't call her your mom since Liv gave birth to you. She's your mom. But your aunt Jade, she's a special woman. She went through a lot to help bring you into this world. And your mom, she's going through a lot too. But when she comes home, she'll be better than ever." At least he hoped so.

He couldn't help but have the same fears Jade had. What if Liv relapsed? What if raising triplets on her own proved to be too much? Jade's lifestyle and work schedule didn't mesh well with raising children. She'd even admitted to not wanting kids of her own. And neither did he. But once he retired from bull riding next year wouldn't he have the time for a family?

Wes rocked back on his heels. What the hell was he thinking? He'd never planned on having kids and even if he had, his daughters weren't his to raise. Liv didn't want him parenting her children. She'd made that painfully clear when she proposed the idea. Up until that point, he had only casually mentioned not wanting kids. So when Liv became adamant about him not being in the girls' lives, it hurt. Not because he wanted to be a father. But because she thought so little of him. The fact she had been hurt and shocked when he moved away had surprised him. How could she have expected them to stay friends? In the back of his mind, he'd wondered if Liv would try to rekindle her relationship with Kevin once the babies were born. Even more reason for her to be happy he was gone. The Liv he knew had become a walking contradiction.

Wes ran his fingers lightly over the bottoms of Audra's feet. "Are you ticklish yet?" Her big blue eyes reflected innocence at its purest. "There's a big world out there waiting for you to conquer it." Her little legs kicked, and he noticed her foot was marker free. "Did your aunt Jade finally figure out how to tell you apart? I always knew. Yes, I did." He lifted her into his arms. "And I'll always remember you as being my first daughter to smile at me."

A tear rolled down his cheek, and he quickly wiped it away. Contrary to what his former ex-best friend thought, Wes enjoyed being around kids. He adored Harlan's eight-year-old daughter, Ivy, and a good 50 percent of his job at the rodeo school in Texas involved him training young children to compete.

Liv had insulted him when she'd assumed it wouldn't bother him to run into his own kids. If that hadn't screamed how she really saw him, he didn't know what would. In hindsight, that should have been his sign to turn Liv down. If she had used an anonymous donor, they could have stayed friends after he moved. Instead he chose to sacrifice it all to give his friend what she wanted most in this world. A known biological father to her children, even though he was technically unnamed.

None of what he did changed how much he hated the idea of marriage and settling down. That had more to do with his parents' dysfunctional marriage. A detail his brothers managed to leave out whenever they remembered the good times. A fight usually followed every one of those good times. Ironically, the only brother who understood was the one who had killed their father.

"You're going to have the best life. Even if I can't be here to see it, I'll make sure you're okay. Better than okay. Think of me as your fairy godfather. I'll always watch over you."

As the girls began to fall asleep, Wes attempted to figure out the logistical nightmare of getting three infants off the floor and down the hall into their bassinets. "How did Liv do this?"

He wished he had thought to bring the car seats in from the mudroom. It would have made baby transport much easier. That reminded him. He needed to install the car seat bases into Jade's rental car. Would they all fit side by side? Two yes, three…no way. Liv had talked about leasing a large SUV but he didn't know what she had eventually chosen.

He tugged out his phone and one-hand typed a quick text message to Jade.

Swing by rental car company after attorney. Need a larger vehicle to fit three infant seats in one row.

Since he wouldn't be around much this weekend, he wanted Jade prepared for any emergency. She and Maddie didn't need to fumble with fastening the seats into two cars if the unexpected happened. He'd take the vehicle down to the sheriff's department and have Harlan or one of the other deputies double-check he'd installed the seats properly. Besides, it would give him a chance to explain his disappearance to his brothers. By now they had probably assumed he was shacked up with one of his old girlfriends while he was in town. If it hadn't been for Jade, he would've been. Unfortunately, for the past two nights, she'd taken center stage in his dreams.

That wouldn't have been a bad thing if he hadn't still resented her for the pain she'd caused him in school. He understood her reason now, and he felt horrible for the role he had played, but it hadn't lessened the damage she'd done. He had been beaten up many times in the locker room after she'd spread around that he had used her as a front because he was gay. The rumor had followed him on the high school rodeo circuit and home. While his brothers only ribbed him about it in the beginning, his father had taken the rumor as gospel and had berated him daily. Her lie had made it impossible for a friend of his to come out because he feared the same treatment from their classmates. Her cruelty had affected far more than just his life. The sad part was, he had started their feud.

After opting to use the bouncy chairs, he successfully made it into the downstairs nursery. Then a whiff of something rotten almost caused him to gag. "What is that?" He covered his nose. "Did something crawl in here and die?" He quickly scanned the room and inspected each crib. "I can't leave you girls in here." He slid their bouncy chairs into the hallway and the odor followed them. Hadley kicked her little legs and made a sour face. "Is that smell coming from you?" He leaned closer and gave her the stiff test, almost passing out in the process. "Oh, that's just not right. How can someone so small and beautiful smell so rotten?"

After changing Hadley's diaper, he decided he'd be proactive and change the other two, just in case. By the time he'd settled them down for a nap, he needed one himself. He also needed to fumigate the room. Located in the back corner of the house, the nursery's open windows offered a nice cross breeze. Northwest Montana got hot in the summer, but most of the time they didn't need to run air-conditioning.

Unwilling to leave them alone in the room, Wes eased into the antique rocking chair in the corner. He ran his hands over the worn wood. He had been with Liv when she stumbled upon it at the county yard sale. He never imagined sitting in it and watching his children sleep. Now he didn't want the moment to end.

Chapter Five

Other than the few minutes he'd spent with Jade when she returned from the attorney's office yesterday, he hadn't seen her or the girls. Maddie had stepped in his place as soon as she'd gotten off work last night. He hadn't even been able to say goodbye when he dropped off Jade's new rental SUV after he had the car seats inspected at the sheriff's department. He'd phoned Jade twice, but she kept reiterating she had it covered and she didn't need him. Once again, he felt cut out of the triplets' lives. And while that had been the original plan, he didn't like it so much now.

Watching Harlan and Dylan stand up as godfather for each other's children left him a little sad and lonely. Three of his brothers had kids—five among them— yet they'd never asked him to be a godfather. Dylan and Garrett had done it twice. That just showed how his brothers saw him. He guessed he couldn't blame them. His reputation had been far from stellar and he had begun to distance himself from them after their father's death. They were always cordial to each other and even joked around some, but the closeness they had once shared continued to fade. Harlan had made more of an effort recently, but now it was too late for Wes to stay in Saddle Ridge. Even if he wanted to be the girls' father, Liv didn't want that. And he couldn't risk his heart breaking every time he ran into them.

When he had stood in the church earlier, he envisioned Audra, Hadley and Mackenzie's christening. Who would be their godparents? He assumed Jade, but who else? And why was he jealous of a man he didn't even know. Did Liv even plan on having them christened? Maybe they had been already. As much as he wanted to know the answers, he knew he had no right to them. And that stung. His brain wanted him to admit that Jade was doing the right thing by keeping him away, but his heart told him otherwise.

"Okay." Harlan wrapped an arm around Wes's shoulder and steered him away from the other christening guests mingling around the Silver Bells Ranch. "It's time you tell me what's really going on."

"What are you talking about?" Wes attempted to shrug him off, but his brother refused to lessen his grip.

"For starters, you showed up without a date. You rarely come to dinner without one, let alone a big event. And something seemed off with that whole car seat situation yesterday."

And here Wes had thought his brother would commend him for putting the children's safety first. "I told you the truth. Liv's sister is here watching the kids."

"I get that. But why isn't Jade using Liv's car and where is Liv anyway?"

Wes faced his brother. "Look, if I tell you, I don't

want it to go any further. Not that it won't be public knowledge at some point anyway. For now, I'd appreciate you keeping this quiet."

For the next half hour, Wes explained the circumstances surrounding Liv's disappearance, conveniently leaving out his role in the triplets' parentage. "And because of my friendship with Liv, Jade asked me for some help. Now that she knows her sister is safe, she's trying to make the best of a very difficult situation. I'm here, so I agreed to pitch in whenever she needs me."

"After Molly walked out on me and Ivy, I had questioned if she had postpartum depression and if I had missed it."

"Wasn't Ivy a year old?"

"If untreated, it can manifest into other disorders. When Molly finally returned, she told me how unhappy she had been in our marriage and that she hadn't been prepared to have a child. To this day I still wonder if PPD played a part in her disappearance. And she had disappeared just like Liv. Only Molly was gone for years. Liv had the sense of mind to get help."

"But Molly's fine now, right?" Ivy's mother had popped back into their lives last year shortly after Harlan and Belle's wedding. Liv's baby drama had just begun to grab hold of Wes at the time and he had selfishly ignored what was going on in everybody else's lives.

"Molly's great. Her relationship with Ivy is still strained, but she missed seven years of her daughter's life. It's a work in progress. And I can't say for sure that she had PPD. I don't think she could, either. But I can tell you Liv is not alone. I've gone on more than a few calls relating to the baby blues as some people ignorantly refer to them. The baby blues and postpartum depression are two different things."

"I saw that mentioned on a few websites too. I watched the girls alone for a few hours when Jade met with the attorney yesterday, and it was overwhelming to say the least."

"I think it's hard for people who've never carried a child—both men and women—to understand all the changes a woman's body goes through postpregnancy. Physical and emotional. Personally, I find the entire process fascinating and beautiful. Granted, I haven't always felt that way. I made a point to be home for a month after Travis was born so I have a better appreciation for it this time around. I can thank Molly for that."

"I didn't realize you and your ex had become such good friends." Wes hated the growing distance between him and his brothers. He and Harlan especially. Wes was a little less than a year older and they'd always been close. But ever since Ryder accidentally killed their father, he'd found it next to impossible to escape their family's dysfunctional past. His brothers' memories differed widely from his because they'd either chosen to ignore it or they'd been that oblivious. Ryder had understood. Until the night he'd made the Slade family the talk of the town. Now that distance seemed impossible to close.

"I don't think Molly and I will ever be good friends." Harlan laughed. "Let's just say we have a newfound respect for one another. She pointed out how absent

I had been when she had Ivy. Liv carried triplets, almost to term if memory serves me correctly. Her body alone had a lot to recover from. It's too bad she didn't have a partner supporting her through all of this. Kevin would have made a great dad if he hadn't turned out to be such a jackass."

"She definitely loved him." Wes grabbed two beers from an ice-filled horse trough and handed Harlan one.

"He loved her, just not enough." Harlan twisted the cap off his beer. "He's getting married sometime next month."

"You're kidding." Wes had only been gone for six months and the Kevin he knew had been loving the single life when he ran into him on New Year's Eve. "To who?"

"Some woman from Kalispell. I haven't met her personally, but I hear she's nice. She has a couple kids from a previous marriage."

Wes froze, the bottle halfway to his mouth. "Wait a minute. That SOB divorced Liv because he didn't want to raise another man's kid and he's marrying someone with kids?" Wes had to tell Jade.

"Yep." Harlan took a long tug of his beer. "In all fairness to Kevin, I think there's a difference between watching your wife carry and give birth to a stranger's child versus coming into the picture years after the fact."

"Still, that had to have hit Liv hard. You wouldn't happen to know when they got engaged, do you?"

Harlan removed his hat and wiped his brow with the back of his arm. "Not sure, but I received the wed-

ding invite probably a month ago. I'm surprised you
didn't get one. They just about invited the entire town.
I think it's still in the envelope it came in. I can check
the postmark when I get home. You think this was a
trigger, don't you?"

"Amongst other things." Wes had read the risk for
postpartum depression increased when the woman
had a weak support system, had difficulty in breast-
feeding, relationship problems and stressful events in
their life. Those are just the things Wes knew Liv had
battled. He loved his friend dearly, but she wasn't ready
to be a single parent. And certainly not a single parent
of three children. He should have said no. "Excuse me
for a second while I call Jade and fill her in."

"Fine, but don't run off somewhere tonight." Harlan
clapped him on the back. "We have a lot of celebrating
to do and you're a part of it. You've been gone for too
long. It hasn't been the same around here without you."

Wes's head started to pound with guilt. He doubted
Dylan or Garrett would take the time to visit him in
Texas. He could already hear the excuses about how
they were too busy running Silver Bells. Even though
Harlan had stuck his head in the sand right beside their
brothers, he desperately tried to keep what was left of
their family together. Surely Harlan, Belle and the kids
would spend the holidays with him in Texas. Of course,
it wouldn't be every year, but maybe every other one.
Despite the past, his chest ached, already longing for
the family events he'd miss.

"I didn't want to say anything earlier in front of
Dylan and Garrett because I was afraid it would start

an argument, but where's Mom?" She hadn't visited after either of Holly's or Travis's birth and now she'd missed the christenings. "This is the first time in years that all of us are together and she can't drag herself away from her new family and precious California to see us. Ryder killed Dad. Why is she punishing us?"

Wes competed in the Golden State a few times a year, and during the rare times his mother made an appearance at one of his events, she brought along her new husband and his adult children. What should have been a nice visit always turned into Wes feeling like an outsider with his own mother.

"We asked her to come and Dylan sent her a wedding invite. She responded tentatively. Considering she missed this weekend, I'd wager a guess that she'll miss the wedding next Saturday." Harlan turned away and watched Belle sitting under one of the ranch's shade trees breast-feeding Travis. She caught his gaze and smiled. Their love for one another radiated across the pasture. Wes had been so hell-bent on never getting himself tied down, that he hadn't given much thought to the sweeter side of marriage. He'd never even come close to that level of commitment with anyone.

"You're a lucky man." Jade's face clouded his vision. No! Jade would not become the first, either. He took a swig of beer. "Let me make this call and I'll catch up with you in a minute."

"Sure thing." Harlan's eyes remained transfixed on Belle as he hopped the top fence rail and walked toward his wife and baby. A love like that was rare. Just because three of his brothers had stumbled upon it over the past year didn't mean anything. They were meant to be family men. He wasn't.

He pulled Jade's number up on his phone and tapped the Call button, praying she'd shoot him straight to voice mail.

"Hello?" Her voice, sultry and deep, reverberated in his ear. Good Lord! One word, two syllables and he was already a goner.

"It's Wes. I'm sure you're busy, but I had to tell you what I just heard about Kevin."

"Kevin? As in my sister's Kevin?"

"As in someone else's Kevin. He's getting remarried. The invites went out about a month ago."

Jade sighed through the phone. "That had to have stung. I wonder why Maddie didn't mention it."

"Maddie moved to town after the divorce. She doesn't know Kevin and I doubt Liv would have mentioned the wedding to her."

"I wish she had confided in me."

"If I hadn't left, I'm positive she'd have told me." Wes chose his next words carefully, not wanting Jade to feel bad about her strained relationship with Liv. "The circumstances surrounding my friendship with your sister leant itself to many all-night discussions about her ex and my family. I moved away, but I should have stayed in contact with her. I own that. That being said, I think this goes beyond Kevin getting married again. His fiancée has kids, so—"

"That jerk!" Jade shouted into the phone. "So he'll be their stepfather."

"You see where I'm going with this, right?"

"My poor sister. She battled everything silently. I shouldn't be surprised. She always has."

"What do you mean?" Once again, the Liv who'd been his friend for almost five years and Jade's version of the same woman were two very different people. She'd been raw and honest, and their talks had been extremely therapeutic and cathartic. If something had bothered her, she'd told him.

"We bounced around a lot when we were kids. Whenever our mom got out of jail and claimed us—" Jade snorted "—as if we were a piece of luggage, Liv became the parent. Constantly babysitting Mom and trying to keep us safe. Between cleaning up drug paraphernalia and hiding our mother's own money so she couldn't blow it all, she took the brunt of the abuse. But I never heard her complain. Not once."

"No child should ever be subjected to that."

"Just like no teenager should have endured the teasing you did because of me. I didn't want to do this over the phone, but I can't wait any longer to apologize to you. I'm sorry."

"That's it? That's all you have to say?" Wes turned away from prying eyes and walked toward the stables as he fought to keep his voice low despite the resentment bubbling beneath the surface. "I understand your grudge against me and I admit, I was wrong to do what I did. But, sweetheart, what you did was a lot more than teasing. You telling everyone I was gay not only got me beat up at school, it followed me on the rodeo circuit and home. Dammit!" Wes tripped and caught himself before he hit the ground. He couldn't walk as fast as he wanted to run. Hell, he wanted to fly far and fast. He unlatched the tack room door and swung it wide. Cradling his phone between his chin and shoulder, he grabbed a saddle and blanket off the wall racks.

"Wes, I—"

"My father looked at me with disgust." Wes interrupted whatever excuse she had in her arsenal. He had to finally tell her how she'd ruined his life. "I won't repeat some of the names he called me, but your little game incited fights at home. Not only between me and my dad. But between my parents because my mom defended me. My dad could be a loving man, but he could also be a bigot. You have no idea what that did to us. What *you* did to us."

"I didn't—" Jade swore under her breath. "I never told anyone you were gay."

"The hell you didn't."

"Wes, please hear me out," Jade pleaded.

Wes held the phone from his ear, tempted to hang up. "Wes?"

"Fine." He had no idea what compelled him to give her a chance to explain, because there couldn't possibly be any justification for her cruelty. "Go for it."

Jade sighed heavily. "I was labeled a slut after you told everyone we had slept together. After everything I'd been through, that really hurt. Here I was the new kid and I already had a reputation for something I didn't do. One afternoon when I was changing for gym class a few girls started calling me names. I wasn't going to take that, so I stood up for myself and I told them we never slept together, and that you had broken up with me because I wasn't your type."

Wes scoffed. He didn't even know what his type was back then. "That's not what I heard."

"I know. One of the girls had twisted my words and inferred that I was saying you were gay. All I wanted to do was get out of that damn locker room, so I didn't respond. By the end of class, the rumor had spread and instead of correcting it and telling everyone that wasn't what I'd meant, I said nothing." Her voice broke. "My silence perpetuated the rumor and for that I'm truly sorry. If I had known what was going on with you at home, I swear I would have been there telling your father it wasn't true."

Tension eased from his jaw as the anger began to slip away. "Even after what I had done to you?"

"Yes. No one deserves what you endured." Her voice soft, barely above a whisper. "My assistant and truly my best friend, Tomás, is gay. He's told me some horrific stories about how he'd been treated when people learned of his sexuality. I would never wish that on my worst enemy. I'm sorry. I realize that doesn't mean much today, but, Wes, I am so sorry for not setting the record straight from the beginning."

For years, he had wanted to rip into Jade and tell her exactly how he felt. To force her to see how bullying affects not only the person being bullied, but everyone around them. While she was wrong to let the rumor get out of hand, he was just as much to blame. He'd lied and told one person they'd slept together, and she'd paid a steep price. If he'd kept his mouth shut and his pride at bay, she'd never have been in the position to defend herself and the escalation wouldn't have happened. They'd both suffered greatly at the hands of the other.

"Wes, are you still there?"

He entered Bonsai's stall, and rested his head against the quarter horse's neck. The animal bobbed his head and nickered, welcoming the human contact.

"Honestly, Jade, I get it. I know all too well how easy it is to lose control of a situation. I also need to accept my part in this. What was it we learned in physics class? For every action there is an equal and opposite reaction. I don't know if you'll ever be able to forgive me. I certainly don't expect it, but I—" Wes swallowed hard at the words he never thought he'd say. "I forgive you. I think we need to put our resentment aside and end this here."

Silence echoed through the phone for a long moment before she spoke. "End this? You make it sound like we won't see you again."

"You made it very clear last night and earlier when I called that I'm not needed. The girls are in very capable hands. But I wish you had come to this realization before you involved me in their lives. I can't unsee what I've already seen. I can't unfeel what's already in my heart."

"You need to spend time with your family. I believe that even more now than I did before. And I'm sorry for getting you involved, but come on, Wes, we were already involved. Who else could I have turned to? You were the only person who knew everything."

"Almost everything. I didn't know about you."

"And your reaction to the news was justified. You told me your initial connection to my sister was misery loves company. I can relate. I didn't want to be alone. I wanted someone who understood. Someone in the same position I'm in. Maddie—" Jade lowered her voice to a whisper. "She's a great help, but she doesn't get it the way you do. I saw that you were struggling with this so I set you free. I don't know what the right thing to do is."

"The right thing is to say goodbye." Wes blinked away the moisture forming in his eyes as he smoothed the saddle blanket over Bonsai's back. "It's better this way."

"Wes—" Her voice was barely audible.

"Goodbye, Jade." Wes disconnected the call and turned off his phone before shoving it in his pocket. He lifted the saddle on the horse and tightened the cinch straps. Nothing cleared a man's mind like being alone with his horse. And since his Tango was in Texas, his uncle's beloved horse was the perfect stand in.

He slid his boot in the stirrup and swung his other leg up over the saddle. He took the reins and exhaled, already feeling like he'd made the right decision to walk away.

A few days ago he'd been itching to jump on the next plane out of town. Now the thought left him empty. He wanted to see his brothers' children grow up. To be there for their birthdays, Thanksgiving, Christmas or whatever special event they had going on. But in doing so, he'd see Audra, Hadley and Mackenzie. He'd have to. He wouldn't be able to stay away and he didn't want to confuse them. He needed to stay anonymous, for their sake and his.

THE HOUSE WAS quiet except for the sound of Jade's fingers tapping on her laptop keyboard. The girls had a 2:00 a.m. feeding a little over an hour ago and had fallen asleep shortly afterward. Even with Maddie's help, Jade struggled to get work done. Two days had passed since she'd last spoke with Wes, three days since she'd seen him. It felt more like a month. She'd promoted Tomás, giving him authority to run the office and hire two more employees. They'd lost a couple lucrative clients over the weekend because Jade wasn't personally there to oversee their event planning. No amount of video chats made up for one-on-one client relations. Tomás was good, probably even better than she was at the job. She had faith in him.

She'd confided in him about how she had severely affected Wes's life. And Tomás pulled no punches when he told Jade that her silence had been just as damaging as if she had actually said the words. He also told her to forgive herself. She laughed at the mere thought. Forgiveness had to be earned and she'd done nothing to deserve it.

Jade slammed her laptop closed and spun around in Liv's übercomfortable office chair. Her purse and keys hung on the door handle, mocking her. She hadn't left the house since her trip to the attorney's office on Friday. Three days. Well, technically four since the night had already crossed into Tuesday. She'd never been that reclusive. Not even when she had the flu last year. She wanted to go for a ride. Not a long one. Just long enough to feel like she'd really gotten out of the house. What if Maddie woke up? What if the girls woke up? And what if they didn't?

Jade grabbed her bag and tiptoed to the back door before she realized Maddie's car blocked hers in the driveway. Crap! Normally she parked at her own house next door, but Maddie had gone grocery shopping after work and it had been easier to park closer and carry the bags into the house. She turned to head back into the office when she noticed Maddie's car keys on the counter. She could move the car, or…she could borrow it. It was borrowing, right? After all, it would be more responsible of her to leave behind the vehicle with the infant seats in case of an emergency.

Okay, logic aside, she was about to steal Maddie's car. The need for an escape—however brief—won out. Was this how Liv had felt? Walking out the door was simple when you were alone. She couldn't imagine doing it with three little ones in tow. She still hadn't taken the girls out of the house. That probably wasn't healthy. This was why she needed a nanny. Unfortunately, finding one qualified enough to care for multiples had been challenging. They were in high demand.

Jade removed a pad from the kitchen drawer, wrote Maddie a note and left it on the counter along with the keys to the SUV…just in case she woke up. Easing the door closed behind her, Jade practically skipped down the drive. She glanced up at the nursery window, guilt weighing heavy on her chest. Jade never felt guilty for anything. She was cutthroat in business and her personal life. Yet she'd been back in Saddle Ridge for less than a week and she'd worn guilt like a push-up bra. And it was every bit as restrictive and uncomfortable.

Five minutes into her escape, Jade realized she was on her way to the Silver Bells Ranch. It was the middle of the night—correction, it was the wee hours of the morning and she had no idea where Wes even stayed on the ranch. For all she knew, he could have left early for South Dakota.

Doubt aside, Jade pulled onto the main ranch road. Except for the other day when she'd first confronted Wes, she hadn't been there before. The full moon glinted off the roof of the picturesque three-story log lodge reminiscent of a Thomas Kinkade painting. Beautiful as it was, it didn't take her breath away like the cowboy walking out the front door did. Jade froze, framing Wes in her headlights. Broad shoulders, lean waist, long legs. No man should look that good. He approached the car and tapped on the passenger window.

"Are you looking for the Silver Bells Ranch lodge?" he asked as she reluctantly lowered the window. "Jade, what are you doing here?"

She groaned, uncertain of the answer herself.

"Is this Maddie's car?"

He leaned in the window, close enough for her to smell the sharp, clean scent of soap. Had he just showered? Maybe he was returning from a tryst with a ranch guest. She felt heat rise to her cheeks and thanked God the car's dark interior shrouded her embarrassment. Why couldn't she have taken a quick drive into town and back?

"Jade?"

She gripped the steering wheel tighter and braved a glance at him. Between his hat and the darkness, she could barely make out his features. "It was the last vehicle in the driveway, so I borrowed it. I have a lot of work ahead of me tonight and I needed to clear my head for a bit. I pulled in here to turn around. I hadn't expected to see you." *Good Lord, why was she rambling?* "What about you? I'm surprised to see you wandering around this late."

"The ranch still isn't operating with a full staff and I'm trying to fill in wherever I can. It makes for long nights." He tried the door handle. "Can you let me in? I wouldn't mind a lift back to my cabin."

"Um, sure." Jade pressed the lock release and he slid in beside her. His bicep brushed against her arm as he set his hat on the dashboard. She now understood the meaning of *compact car*. Mistake number two…she should have flip-flopped vehicles and taken the SUV instead. At least he would've been an arm's length away. "You'll have to tell me where to go."

When he didn't respond, she lifted her gaze to his. The dashboard lights turned his warm hazel eyes a deep, dark chocolate brown, drawing her into their depths. The man was too much, on too many levels. They didn't even like each other, so why the sudden attraction?

Because it wasn't sudden. He had been her first crush fifteen years ago, before he screwed it up. Crush or not, she hadn't been ready for anything sexual back then. She'd spent years hating him, only now she wasn't sure how she felt. Knowing the truth had lessened that hate, if she could even call it hate anymore. That anger had been redirected toward Burke, where it should have been all along. She had no right to feel anything toward Wes except remorse. While she'd endured bullying and slut-shaming for four years, the physical attack had been swift. Wes had endured far more because of her silence.

"I wanted to call you."

Jade rested her head against the seat and laughed. "You're the one who said goodbye."

"That doesn't mean I don't still care."

Jade ignored the sincerity in his voice and shifted the car into Drive. "The girls are fine. I haven't found a nanny yet and there's been no word from Liv or the treatment center."

Wes covered her hand with his. "What about you? How are you doing?"

Jade gripped the gearshift tighter under the heat of his palm. "I, um, I've been busy trying to keep my company going. It's a bit tough to do this far from home."

"I can imagine." He gave her hand a light squeeze before releasing it. "That's quite an operation you have there. I hope you don't mind. I looked you up online."

Nervousness crept into her chest as she shifted the car back into Park. "Hey, it's fair. You already know I looked you up. I noticed you haven't posted any photos for the past few days."

"I haven't been in the mood. I haven't wanted to do much of anything since…since I last saw you." He hooked her chin with his finger, gently forcing her to turn toward him. "You've been on my mind. Constantly."

"We're enemies," she whispered.

"We were enemies." His breath, warm against her cheek, sent a shiver through her body. "We are so much more than that and as hard as I try, I can't forget the lives we've created together, however unknowingly. We will always have that connection and no one can take that from us."

"Wes." Jade choked back a sob. "There's nothing we can do about it. They aren't ours to keep. As much as I fear my sister won't get better, I have to believe she will. We can't acknowledge that they came from us. And nothing can ever come from that connection. Liv didn't want us to know about the other. It was her secret, and a friendship or whatever is impossible."

"Now we can't even be friends?"

Hurt reflected in his eyes and it took every ounce of restraint she had not to touch him and attempt to ease his pain.

"No. The risk is too high. And it would hurt Liv. I still need to find a way to tell her you've seen the girls and have spent time with them. I'll discuss it with her doctor when I visit her. I think it's a big enough problem to warrant a third party. I can't imagine her not being threatened by it."

"No chance of keeping it secret, huh?"

Jade shook her head. "If I never planned to see her again, then maybe. I can't look at my sister and lie though. The truth would come out eventually."

"Let me ask you something." Wes shifted in his seat and leaned against the door. "Twice now you've mentioned the truth coming out. Were you and Jade planning to tell the girls that you're their biological mother?"

"Possibly. It depends on the situation." It broke her heart knowing the girls might one day learn their mother and aunt had lied to them for years. Regardless of how well-intentioned the lie had been. "There are a number of factors I wish I had considered before agreeing to this. It's been a lot harder than I imagined. For all of us."

"I have an idea, but I want you to hear me out before you say no."

"Okay, should I be worried?" She laughed nervously.

"If you moved to the ranch—"

"Are you insane?" He must be to propose the one thing that would send her sister into orbit. "Absolutely not."

His brow furrowed. "It's a good idea if you'll let me finish."

"Okay." Jade bit back a retort and raised her hands in surrender. "Go ahead."

"You obviously feel isolated at Liv's house because you're driving around in the middle of the night. You don't have a nanny or any other help during the day. Now I may not know of any professional child caregivers, but I can personally vouch for many of the teenagers living on this ranch. I've known them their entire lives from when their parents worked on my father's ranch and then came here. They are home from school for the summer, looking to earn some extra cash. I'm sure one or two of them would be more than happy to give up cleaning guest quarters to help you with the girls. The few I have in mind helped raise their little brothers and sisters so they're not inexperienced."

Hiring them wasn't a bad idea. But move to the ranch? No. "Why can't they come out to the house?"

"Because they don't have cars. They would need someone to transport them back and forth. Their parents work, and it would be too much of a strain on you."

Okay, he had a point there. "Your idea has merit, but I think it's better if I wait and find a professional nanny. I'm flattered, but after the things you said the other day, I'm confused why you're asking me to move in with you?"

"You wouldn't be living with me because I won't be here. I head out to South Dakota tomorrow…well I guess it's already tomorrow, but I'll be back in time for the wedding on Saturday. Then I head home to my job and life in Texas."

Jade's stomach knotted at the thought of him leaving. "Do you have a girlfriend waiting for you there too?"

Wes's features softened as a slow smile eased across his face. "Aw, sweetheart." He ran the back of his fingers lightly down her cheek. "I'm flattered by your jealousy, but I am one hundred percent single."

"I am not jealous." She smacked him away.

"Ouch!" He rubbed his hand. "You're cute when you're riled up."

"You are so asking for it." The man infuriated her more than a bridezilla with a bathroom emergency. He also turned her insides to mush. Only he could make her feel like a lovesick teenager again. Not that she was lovesick. *Love* was *evil* spelled backward…okay…misspelled *evil*. Regardless, it was close enough and she wanted no part of it. Love came with attachments and commitments. She had enough of that at work. She was married to her job and that was all she needed. "You can't just install me in the lodge and leave me with a bunch of strangers."

"I was thinking more along the lines of one of the guesthouses that are not in use. My brothers are still rebuilding Silver Bells. Business is much better than it was a year ago, but we're still not fully booked." Wes ran his hands down his thighs and Jade wondered if he was as nervous as she was. "Of course, I would have to discuss it with them first, but I don't see it being a problem. If you're worried about people gossiping about Liv being in a PPD treatment center, I promise you, my family is not like that. Harlan understood and even en-lightened me about a few things."

"You told him?" Jade closed her eyes, silently add-ing one more item to the list of things she had to tell her sister. "Why did you do that? Liv should have an opportunity to say what she does and doesn't want peo-ple to know."

"Harlan didn't give me a choice. He knew something was wrong when I showed up at the sheriff's department with your rental SUV instead of your sister's. I have a hard time lying to my brothers the same way you have a hard time lying to your sister."

"Fine, but I can't move cribs and whatever else I need to your family's ranch."

"We have cribs. Emma—the woman my brother Dylan is marrying on Saturday—wanted families to think of Silver Bells as a second home when they visited. She personally redecorated a few of the larger guest cabins with mothers in mind. We have five brand-new cribs at the ready. Those particular cabins have full kitchens with dishwashers, washing machines and dryers, guest bedrooms, rocking chairs and all the creature comforts of home."

"Wow." She planned events at guest ranches with similar amenities and they didn't come cheap. "Your brothers must have some budget to do all that."

Wes shook his head. "That was all Emma. She bought into the ranch as did many of our employees over the last six months. Silver Bells was on the verge of bankruptcy after my uncle died. Now it's a thriving family and employee-owned business. It still has a way to go, but it's getting great reviews and by next summer there will be a reservation waiting list."

"The way you speak so proudly of the ranch, I'm surprised you aren't a partner."

Wes rested his arm on the open window frame and stared out the windshield. "They asked me, but I think they felt obligated to. I had to say no anyway."

"Because of Mackenzie, Audra and Hadley?" Jade hated how three innocent children were the cause of so much misery. It wasn't fair.

"They were a part of it, but I had already planned to leave. I see my father wherever I go in this town. Some of those memories are really good and others not so much. I hate Ryder for what he did. And I hate my father for the way he treated me. For the way he treated my mom. I hate my mom for leaving and never coming back. She wasn't even at the christenings. Those are her grandchildren, but she couldn't do it."

Jade reached across the armrest and entwined her fingers with his. "Maybe the pain is too much for her to return. The same way you said it would be too painful for you to come back."

"I've told myself that a thousand times. She's remarried and I'm happy for her. I truly am. And please don't get me wrong, as much as I hate some of the things my family has done, they are still my family and I love them with all my heart. Just like I love Audra, Hadley and Mackenzie."

"I think it's impossible not to." Jade wanted to comfort him…to find comfort in him, but the barriers were too great for her to cross.

"I didn't want to. I tried not to. But the truth is, I loved them the minute Liv showed me the ultrasound. Something changed in me that day and I can't explain it." His fingers tightened around hers. "I realize I hurt your sister by severing all ties with her after that, but I was afraid to stay friends. If that was my reaction to a grainy black-and-white photo, I could only imagine what it would be like seeing them once they were born. Let alone in person. And I was right. They took my breath away. I may be heading back to Texas on Sunday, but I will never be the same after these two weeks."

"Neither will I." Jade released him and covered her face with her hands. The tears she had carefully held in check over the past few months finally broke the dam. "I feel so guilty for regretting my decision to do this.

But I would never take it back. I would never trade their lives in for anything."

"I know, honey. I know." Wes wrapped his arm around her shoulders and pulled her to him. "Neither would I."

"How do I do this?" She sobbed against his chest. "And how am I supposed to do it alone?"

"Move in here."

"How can that possibly work? If you see a resemblance between the girls and your nephew, don't you think your family will? Never mind that my sister would freak over the arrangement."

"You're forgetting that one of your sister's best friends is engaged to my brother Garrett. She may notice a resemblance whether you're here or not. Granted your sister had started the process before Delta and Garrett got together so she couldn't have predicted that connection. But she knew about Harlan and Belle's baby because I told her. Harlan told me when Belle was only four weeks along."

"What did she say?" Jade asked against the softness of his shirt.

"She was thrilled for them. A few days later she had our embryos implanted. But she didn't think this through. I have a lot of respect for Liv, but I think she was so in love with the idea of having a baby, she didn't see the whole picture. Like what happens when Travis and her daughters are in the same class together? Someone's bound to comment on the resemblance. What happens if one of those girls wants to date him when they get older? They're cousins. What is she going to do? How will she explain that?"

"Oh my God! I hadn't thought of that." Jade pulled away from him.

"You shouldn't have to."

Wes brushed her hair away from her face, allowing it to fall behind her shoulder. His touch tender and kind, as if they'd actually been friends. She hadn't thought he was capable of so much compassion.

"You were a donor. I was a donor," he continued. "I can't tell you how many times I've replayed that scenario in my head these past couple days. Your sister either has to move out of town, or she needs to face the cold reality that people will discover the truth. As much as I don't want to reveal my role in this, I realize I can only control a part of it."

"That had to have weighed on Liv." People had babies every day without complication, yet Audra, Hadley and Mackenzie were surrounded by it. Any decision she, Wes and Liv made affected them.

"I'm sure it did. It's too big of a secret to bear. Up until five days ago, she was the only one who knew the entire truth."

"It's killing me not to be able to talk to her." Ironic since she had subconsciously avoided speaking with Liv for weeks. "I have so many questions."

"She may not have any answers."

"I got so mad at her this afternoon." Jade hugged her arms to herself. "I lost another major client because I'm not in LA. Tomás is wonderful and I trust him with my life, but I had contracts with people who expected me to handle their events personally. And to a large degree I had. There's a lot I can do remotely, but I can't hold someone's hand through a catering or cake testing or walk them through a venue. My face on Tomás's iPad just wasn't enough to convince them to stay. We had already invested quite a bit of money in this one. I took a big hit."

"That doesn't seem right. Can't you fight that?"

"Sure." Jade bitterly laughed. "And then that celebrity will tell their friends not to use us. LA may be a large city, but it's a small town at heart. Everyone knows everyone else and reputations can be destroyed with one phone call. I have to suck it up." She inhaled deeply. "I'm mad at my sister for putting me in this situation. I'm not mad she has postpartum depression. But let's be honest, she made some big mistakes. And let me tell you, I pass some of that blame on the fertility specialist she went to. Counseling should be mandatory, especially when implanting three embryos in a single mother. I find that irresponsible. So, yeah, I'm mad. And the guilt eats at me for feeling that way because Liv had to be a complete wreck over this."

Wes gathered her into his arms again and held her tightly. "You're human first. That's why I'm asking you to move in here." His voice smooth and insistent as he rested his head on hers. "By staying at Liv's you're doing exactly what she did. Let me and my family help you. And if they figure out the truth, we'll handle it then. Hopefully it won't come to that. Don't wait until you're so strung out, both emotionally and financially, to do something."

"What about Maddie? She's personally invested in this. She loves the children."

"She should come with you so you're not alone at night."

Because you'll be in Texas. Jade wanted to be selfish and ask him to stay. A small part of her loved the connection they shared. Wes Slade, of all people, was the one person who completely understood. The pretense had slipped away and she wanted nothing more than to lean on him for support.

She lifted her head from his chest and looked into his eyes. Could she really put the past aside and trust him?

"Maybe moving here isn't such a bad idea. But it's only temporary."

Wes cupped her chin, his mouth inches from hers. "It's going to be okay. I'll talk to my brothers and we'll figure this out. Together."

"Together?" Jade had never yearned to kiss a man so badly. "But you're leaving."

"I'll call you every day." He stroked her cheek, brushing away what remained of her tears. "You'll still have me."

If only she had him... Her sister would never forgive her. Jade sat up straight and gripped the steering wheel. "Okay, um, yeah, talk to your brothers and we'll take it from there. How about you show me where to drop you off."

Wes cleared his throat and adjusted his jeans. "Make a left at the stables and follow that road to the end."

Jade shifted the car into gear and stepped on the gas.

The engine revved, but didn't move. "Please tell me I didn't break Maddie's car."

"Try putting it in Drive instead of Neutral." Wes laughed under his breath.

Jade stared down at the glowing *N* on the shifter. What was it about Wes? She took pride in always remaining in control, yet whenever she was around him, she made a fool of herself. He was charming, thoughtful, handsome—okay, downright sexy—but he was off-limits. A relationship, even a fleeting, one-night sexual one, was out of the question with the father of her children.

Damn.

She braked the car abruptly in front of his cabin. "Get out."

Wes laughed, making no move to open the door.

Jade flipped up the armrest and reached across his lap for the door handle, pushing it open. "Get out before I do something we'll both regret."

Before she could retreat to her side of the car, he gripped her waist and tugged her onto his lap, the full extent of his arousal evident against her hip. "What if we don't regret it?"

"We can't." She splayed her hands on his chest and pushed away from him, her back against the dashboard.

"Because you don't want to, or because of your sister?"

"Oh, I definitely want to." Her eyes wandered down his abs to his belt buckle as his thumb grazed the side of her breast. In seconds, she could have his jeans unzipped and end the tension between them. She closed her eyes, relishing the thought. She'd never understood that deep sexual yearning she'd heard her brides talk about…until now. A shrink once told her it had been because of her past. She'd always believed she just hadn't met the right man yet. But despite the unfamiliar desire raging deep within her, she couldn't betray her sister any more than she was already.

"We can't do this to Liv. It's not fair to her."

"Okay." He nodded silently and released her. "Just for the record, I don't think it's fair that your sister gets to dictate how we feel about each other." Wes reached for the door. "Before I say any more, I'm going to go take a cold shower."

Jade slid back to her side of the car. "You and me both."

"We could always take one together." Wes snatched his hat from the dashboard. "But then we'd get all steamy again. Good night, Jade. I'll call you after I speak to my brothers." He stepped out of the car and closed the door, giving her a pleasant view of his backside in the process. He leaned in the window before walking away. "Sweet dreams, sweetheart."

"You too."

"I do believe you're blushing."

"Good night, Wes."

Jade pulled away from the cabin before he tempted her further. If he could melt her resolve without even kissing her, she could only imagine what would happen to her if he did. Wes was right, he needed to go back to Texas. She was safer that way.

Chapter Six

Jade stepped outside the large log guest cabin and admired the rising sun over the Swan Range. Okay, maybe Wes was right, the view was photoworthy. She sipped her mug of coffee as Belgian horses grazed lush green grass in the corral twenty yards from the expansive wraparound porch. Dylan and Garrett had been gracious enough to offer her the place for free, but she refused. She could afford to pay their more than reasonable rate, although a part of her wondered if they had discounted the cost. Wes had been insistent on paying the entire bill, but Jade relented and allowed him to share half the expense.

Wes had only been gone a day, and she surprisingly missed him. The ranch, vast as it was, seemed empty without him there. Not that they had spent any time there together, except for the day she arrived and their heated exchange in Maddie's car.

She glanced over at the maroon Ford parked alongside the cabin. Her body began to tingle at the memory. She'd almost had sex with Wes Slade in the front seat of a car. What the hell was happening to her? They weren't in high school. Regardless, the man had already affected Jade and the girls. He hadn't been a part of their lives for very long, but the triplets seemed more content and settled when he was around. Nothing would replace their mother though.

For infants, they'd had so many changes in their little lives and Jade was grateful Maddie agreed to stay at the ranch with her. She had been their one constant. It also didn't hurt that the woman had a major crush on a ranch hand she met at the christenings who just happened to live on the other side of the property.

"Here you are," Maddie said from the open doorway. "Wow. That view's worth a million bucks and then some."

"Are the girls awake yet?"

"Not yet." She padded barefoot to the railing and inhaled the fresh scent of morning dew. "This has to be the first night they've slept more than four hours in a row."

"Maybe it's the country air." Jade had the best sleep of her life after feeding and putting the triplets to bed around two thirty. "I should brace myself for the dirty diaper onslaught while you get ready for work."

"I don't know." Maddie, still in her sleep shorts and T, flopped into one of the porch rocking chairs and closed her eyes. "I may play hooky today and just admire the landscape."

"You mean admire Jarrod."

Maddie glared at her and narrowed her eyes. "Do you see Jarrod anywhere, because I don't."

"No, but I'm sure you'll know his schedule by tonight. And if you get dressed fast enough, you can catch him at the breakfast buffet up at the main lodge."

"Really?" Maddie shot upward. "I mean, breakfast sounds like a good idea."

Jade stifled her laughter as Maddie ran back inside the cabin. She wished she had a friend like Maddie in LA. Tomás and his husband were always around for business or pleasure, but Jade felt like a third wheel whenever they went out together. Her social calendar was packed almost every night so she couldn't complain, but most of those events were business related in some way. She had to out-network the competition to remain relevant, which didn't leave much time for dating.

"Good morning!" A woman called out from an ATV as she drove up to the porch. "It's refreshing here, isn't it?"

The voice and the face were familiar, but Jade couldn't place the woman. Then the realization hit her. "Delta?"

"I know, I look different with a pixie cut, but I didn't have much say in that." She eased off the ATV and unfastened a large tote from the back before climbing the steps. "How are you? I'm sorry I wasn't around when the babies were born."

Jade gave the woman a hug, then held her at arm's length. "Wow! You look amazing." Delta had been stunning before, but her deep mahogany close-cropped hair accented her slender neck, perfect breasts and mile-long legs. "You look more like a supermodel than someone recovering from cancer."

"Well, thank you." Delta mock-strutted a mini catwalk and spun around. "Cancer forces you to take better care of yourself. Besides eating healthier, I'm working out more and kicking some major butt. Life's too short not to. I'm really sorry to hear about Liv. I wish I could have been around more during her pregnancy."

"No, no, please. You had your own struggles. I get it."

Delta nodded, her eyes brimming with tears.

"I have something for you." She held up the bag. "Belle—Harlan's wife—has been teaching me how to bake whole grain bread and muffins, so our kitchen is overflowing with all sorts of yumminess. I thought you and Maddie would like some."

"Absolutely. She's inside getting ready for work."

"Ready for work or ready for *Jarrod*?" She fanned herself as she said his name.

"Oh, you know, huh?"

"Honey, I had a ringside seat to the drool fest. And yes, dear Maddie was drooling."

"Why don't you come in and you can tell me about it over coffee." Jade opened the screen door and held it for Delta. "We may actually get a chance to talk before the girls wake up."

Delta followed her to the large family-sized eat-in kitchen. Jade loved the cabin's thoughtful little details, like easy-to-sterilize solid core countertops and child safety latches on all the cabinets, top and bottom in case someone's child was a climber.

"Besides wanting to pawn my food off on you, I sort of have a favor to ask."

"Okay." Jade poured two mugs of hot coffee and set them on the table. "Do you take cream or sugar?"

"Just black, thank you."

Jade peered into the tote and pulled out a bag of blueberry muffins. "Oh, these look amazing," she said before taking a bite. "These are incredible. I love the addition of the orange zest. It really brightens the flavor."

"I thought so too. Normally you see lemon and blueberry paired together, but the orange is a nice citrus twist."

"I'm sorry. I guess I'm hungrier than I thought." Jade wiped her fingers on a napkin. "Please ask me the favor."

"Um, okay." Worry lines creased Delta's forehead as she death-gripped her mug. "I'm sure you can imagine the first half of the year was really rough for Garrett, me and the kids."

Jade reached across the table and covered her hands. "What is it? Did something else happen?"

"It's nothing bad at all." Delta's caramel-brown eyes met hers. "It's just a big favor to ask. June has been our turning point of sorts. I'm done with chemo, my scans look great and we can finally move on with our lives."

"I have an idea where this is going." Jade hoped she was correct.

Delta returned her enthusiasm. "Garrett and I have been talking and we really want to get married this summer. The problem is, the kids leave to visit their grandparents in Wyoming on Monday, and they won't be back for a month which would give us more than enough time to squeeze in a honeymoon. It's important his kids are in the ceremony, so eloping is out of the question."

"And you want to have the wedding this week."

Delta's smile widened. "After the christenings on last Saturday, we asked Dylan and Emma if they would mind us getting married this weekend too. We thought it would be the perfect time since many of the same people we'd invite are already in town. They loved the idea."

"I'm so happy for you!" Jade gave Delta another hug. "Dylan and Emma have their wedding planned and set for Saturday afternoon and the reception goes into the evening. We don't want to disrupt that, but we also realize that many people are flying or driving home on Sunday. We just want a simple ceremony, at sunrise Sunday morning and then a quick breakfast reception before everyone leaves."

"It sounds wonderful. I'm jealous I haven't thought of that idea before. I've planned a lot of double ceremonies, but yours is a much better idea. One wedding doesn't encroach on the other."

"Exactly. And we'd each have our own anniversary date."

"So." Jade folded her arms over her chest. "Are you going to ask me or what?"

"Okay." Delta beamed. "I know you're super busy with the triplets and your company in LA, but would you be willing to help plan our wedding? I realize it's only four days away, but—"

"But nothing. I would love to." This was the pick-me-up Jade needed. To physically get her hands on a project instead of doing it remotely. "I have a ton of ideas already."

"We're on a tight budget though." Delta winced. "I

know you do big, lavish Hollywood ceremonies. That's just way out of our reach."

"You'd be surprised how many celebrities want small weddings. My assistant had an intimate ceremony last year, and it meant so much more than the bigger ones." Jade lowered her voice to a whisper. "But don't tell anyone I said that. It would kill my business."

"I promise I won't." Delta giggled. "I feel bad that Liv won't be here for it though."

"Liv's happy if you're happy. I won't even tell her when I see her. I'll leave that for you."

Delta nodded. "Thank you for doing this for us. One more thing, my dog Jake has to be in the ceremony. I can't get married without him."

"You're welcome and I've added many dogs to wed—" The sound of one baby, followed by another, rang out from down the hall. "They're playing my song. I think Emma had the right idea putting us so far away from the main lodge."

"It's loud when there's three of them, isn't it?" Delta stood with Jade. "Do you mind if I help? I haven't seen them in a month."

"Sure." Jade swallowed hard, hoping Delta didn't pick up on the similarities between the girls and Travis, especially Mackenzie. "Just be forewarned, they can pack an odoriferous punch."

"Oh!" Delta waved her hand in front of her face as they entered the bedroom. "That they do. Chemo annihilated my sense of smell and taste buds, but I'll tell ya, I can definitely smell that. Is that normal?"

"For Stinker One, Two and Three, yes. Wes said Travis's was slightly better, but not by much. I don't know if it's their formula or what. They have a two-month checkup at the pediatrician's next week, and it's at the top of my list."

"Oh hey, Delta." Maddie wrinkled her nose as she entered the room. "Welcome to the danger zone. Enter at your own risk."

"You think after working around horses and their manure for most of my life, a baby would smell like roses. Okay." Delta squared her shoulders. "Where do we begin?"

Jade bet if Delta had goggles and a hazmat suit, she'd have put it on. "Neither one of you need to help me. Go get some breakfast and ogle your men."

"Nonsense." Delta hip checked Jade out of the way. "Three babies, three of us. Let's do this before they claim a victim."

As if on cue, Audra, Hadley and Mackenzie stopped and stared up at the women laughing at them for a brief second before continuing to cry.

"Oh, did we insult you?" Maddie lifted Audra out of the crib. "We're sorry. Just like Aunt Jade is sorry she labeled you with a Sharpie when she first got here."

"You did what?" Delta's eyes widened at she lifted Mackenzie.

"Ah, I'll take her." Jade eased the infant out of Delta's arms. She didn't want her getting that up close and personal with the triplet that resembled Travis the most. "Mackenzie's the fussiest."

"She is?" Maddie asked. "Since when?"

Jade scrambled for an excuse. "Monday. You were

at work when I noticed it. I've been double-checking to make sure she doesn't have a rash or anything. I should have mentioned it before." Jade hated having to lie to the one person who'd been the greatest and most unexpected help to her over the past week.

"I think all three of them have been a little more gassy than usual." Maddie grabbed a diaper blanket from the dresser and knelt on the floor to change Audra, giving Delta the changing table. "Definitely let Alyssa and Megan know when they come today."

Jade had met with two of the sweetest teenage girls after Wes had helped move her onto the ranch. His future sister-in-law, Emma, had personally used them many times and highly recommended them. At first Jade wondered if hiring two people was overkill, but she liked the idea of them having each other for companionship so they wouldn't get bored. Jade needed to devote her full attention to work, and she didn't want to feel compelled to entertain a babysitter.

"Someone please tell me the baby labeling story," Delta asked.

"Maddie will never let me live this down. I was afraid of mixing up the babies so I wrote their first initial on the bottom of their feet."

"With a permanent black marker," Maddie added.

"It washed off...eventually." Jade rolled her eyes. "It's not like I had them tattooed."

"Why didn't you use nail polish?" Delta asked as she changed Hadley.

"Because I thought they'd chew it off."

"Not if you put it on their toes." Delta held her nose

and shoved the offending package in the Diaper Genie. "They're not coordinated enough to reach them."

"In case my sister hasn't told you already…babies were never my thing. Liv wanted a big family. I wanted the big house in the Hollywood Hills."

"And now you have the kids and you're living in a log cabin on a ranch." Delta refastened Hadley's onesie and rubbed her belly. "There you go, little one. All clean and sweet smelling."

"I'm here temporarily," Jade quickly added. "I have a lot invested in my business. I can't be away from it forever. I'm already taking major financial hits after one week."

At least when she had visited Liv when the babies were born that had been planned. Her clients had known in advance she wouldn't be around during those dates, with the understanding Liv could have gone into labor early instead of getting induced. She'd had months to plan for her absence and some clients had even chosen to push their events out so Jade would be in town overseeing them. She couldn't blame them for being furious she was gone again.

"Do I hear someone's phone ringing?" Delta asked.

"That's mine." Her assistant's familiar ringtone beckoned from the kitchen. Jade glanced up at the wall clock. It was shortly after seven and she knew he was eager to go over today's schedule. "It's Tomás. We have a big event tonight."

"On a Wednesday?" Maddie lowered Audra into her crib, then gently nudged Jade out of the way. "Go take your call. I can do this."

"Thanks." She stepped aside and walked toward the bathroom to wash her hands. "Hollywood doesn't care what day it is." The phone stopped ringing, and she envisioned Tomás huffing impatiently as he waited for her outgoing message to finish so he could leave a voice mail. Jade hesitated in the doorway, watching Delta's reaction to the triplets. If she detected any family resemblance, she didn't show it. Then again, don't a lot of babies look similar at that age? Maybe Wes had been overreacting. Maybe they both had been and everything would work out the way Liv had planned.

"WHAT'S WRONG WITH you today?" Wes's agent asked as the medics wheeled him through the arena's corridors and outside to the mobile sports medicine trailer. "Your head clearly wasn't in it. I picked up on that before you ever entered the chute. You blew me off when I asked. I hate to say it, kid, but you seem a little soft this week."

Maybe if he could get the image of Jade sitting on his lap out of his head, he might be able to concentrate. He'd never been more attracted or infuriated by any other woman. And yeah, in a perfect world, he'd like to see where things might lead with her, but their lives were far from perfect. Once he'd explained to his brothers yesterday about Liv's disappearance and asked if Jade and the girls could move to the ranch, it had raised all sorts of questions. Adding Maddie to the mix had been the only reason they stopped. His brothers didn't even think he'd keep two girlfriends in the same house.

"I've been in Montana and I haven't had a chance to ride or work out for over a week." The multimillion-dollar rodeo training facility he taught at in Texas had a top-of-the-line fitness center and both real and mechanical bulls for training. The pay was great, but the perks were even better. He'd taken every advantage of it when he wasn't on the road.

"That's no excuse," Pete argued. "You lived in Montana up until you moved six months ago, and you were fine then."

He was right, and Wes couldn't fight the truth. "Look, man." Wes reached with his good arm and tapped the medic's leg. "I'm fine to walk. I dislocated my shoulder, not my feet."

"You know the rules," the man said without slowing down. "We can't do that in case you have other injuries. Just be glad we didn't take you out strapped to a stretcher."

"Very funny." The dig was a not-so-subtle reference to an injury he had last year during finals. He'd been furious at himself for miscalculating the bull's rotation and wound up unconscious on the arena floor after the animal headbutted him. He knew the second he'd awoken he'd been eliminated from the competition. He'd gone out kicking and screaming louder than Audra, Hadley and Mackenzie.

"What's got you all in knots. Is something going on with your family that I don't know about?"

"You could say that."

"As long as it doesn't involve a woman," Pete scoffed.

"Try four."

"Four what? Four women?" Pete almost tripped over his own feet.

"Right on!" The older medic walking alongside them tried to high-five Wes before realizing he was on his dislocated side. "Whoops, sorry. My bad."

"You've gotten in more trouble with women than anyone I know." Pete clucked his tongue. "Don't let them get in the way of your career."

Once they reached the trailer, Wes insisted on walking up the steps himself. He refused to be wheeled up a ramp despite the medical team surrounding him. After he stripped off his safety vest and shirt, Dr. Shelton began assessing his injuries.

"What's this…your third dislocation in two years?" he asked, reviewing his charts on a tablet. Deceiving from the outside, the forty-foot-long trailers housed state-of-the-art mobile medical centers that traveled nationwide treating sports injuries. Competitors no longer had to go to the emergency room since they could perform everything including X-rays, minor surgery and casting on-site. They were also his largest sponsor and trying to hide any injury was futile.

"Just pop it back in, Doc." Wes ground his back teeth from the pain.

Dr. Shelton handed his tablet to one of the nurses. "You know the drill. Sit up straight and shrug your shoulders." The man gripped Wes's wrist and eased his elbow into a 90-degree angle, keeping it close to his body and in line with his shoulder. He slowly began to rotate the arm outward until the pressure increased on the dislocation. "Now try to relax as much as you can."

"I'm feeling that, Doc." Wes exhaled slowly and looked up at his agent hovering nearby. Pete had helped him build his career from junior rodeo greenhorn to champion, and he hated disappointing the man even more than he hated disappointing himself.

"We're almost there." The doctor gripped his upper arm and slowly moved it out and upward. "Good. Now put your shoulders back, your chest out."

Wes closed his eyes trying to focus on anything other than the pain. He didn't remember any of his other dislocations hurting this bad. Then he heard a pop, and the pain began to subside.

"Keep your back straight. It's not quite all the way in yet," Dr. Shelton said as he rotated Wes's arm toward his chest.

"There we go, there we go." Wes tilted his head back at the release.

"And you're done." The man let go of his arm. "Let's get you into X-rays so we can see what's going on in there."

Wes stood, the tension draining from his shoulder. "I'm fine."

"Look," Pete said, stepping in front of him, "you didn't qualify, so it's not like you're riding again. Let the man do his job."

"I made eight."

"No, Wes. You didn't. Your time was 7.8, and it was a sloppy 7.8."

He missed it by two-tenths of a second. "Dammit." Wes kicked the chair behind him. "I thought I had it." He rarely missed qualifying. His sponsorships were coming up for renewal and a few younger competitors had been slowly pushing him down in the ranks. This was not the time to screw up.

"We'll talk about it later." Pete pulled out his phone and tapped at the screen.

"Come on, Wes. Chaps off, gown on," the doctor ordered.

"Fine."

"I'll be outside waiting." Pete's phone rang, and he was out the door before Wes had a chance to respond.

He unfastened his chaps and kicked off his boots. He suspected Pete was already looking to poach one of the younger riders from the lesser known agents. He may not like it, but he couldn't blame the man. Wes intended to retire at the end of next season, even though he hadn't told anyone of his plans yet. He wanted to have two solid final years and another championship under his belt before then. The higher he went out, the more money he could earn training the next generation of competitors. He had nothing else to fall back on.

After two hours of tests and endless waiting, Dr. Shelton's grim expression told Wes all he needed to know. Controlling the argument building in his head, he sat patiently and listened.

"Three dislocations, extensive ligament damage and now a rotator cuff tear, the only thing I see in your immediate future is surgery."

"No." Wes shook his head. "Absolutely not. I'll just rehab it again. The Ride 'em High! Rodeo School where I work in Texas is connected to the Dance of Hope Hippotherapy Center. They have the best physical therapists in the state. You know the place, Doc, and you know their reputation."

"Tell me something." Dr. Shelton clasped his hands. "On a scale of one to ten, what was your pain level when you rode today?"

"I don't know." Wes had thought the week off from teaching and competition would have given his arm and shoulder a rest. He didn't want to admit defeat. And he wouldn't. Not yet. Besides, it hadn't been bothering him this bad. "Maybe a five, possibly a six."

"Compare that to a year ago. What was your pain level then?"

"None." Wes snorted. "I don't get the question, Doc. I wasn't injured then, so of course it would be zero."

"Exactly. You weren't injured then, now you are."

Wes stood. He didn't appreciate games, let alone one at his expense. "I'm not having surgery."

"What's this about surgery?" Pete asked from the doorway.

Dr. Shelton's brows rose as he stared at Wes. His medical records were private and the man couldn't legally say a word to Pete. But his sponsorship contract stipulated they were to be informed of any and all injuries affecting his ability to compete. In the end, the sponsor would tell Pete and there was no sense in delaying it.

"The good doc is recommending surgery."

"What kind of surgery?"

"We haven't discussed that yet." Dr. Shelton removed his glasses and rubbed his eyes. "Your client refuses to hear what I have to say."

"Because I know you're talking rotator cuff surgery and that will take me out of competition for six months."

"Probably longer," Pete muttered.

"Not happening. At least not now. I choose rehab and at the end of the season, I will have it reevaluated and we'll take it from there."

"That's months away," Dr. Shelton said. "If you have surgery now, you'll have a strong chance of recovering and competing in a full season next year. I can pretty much guarantee that won't happen if you wait much longer. You can't ride without pain."

"I'm tough enough to ride through it."

"Thank you, Dr. Shelton." Pete clapped Wes on the back and gave him a gentle shove toward the door. "We will definitely consider all options."

Wes opened his mouth to argue and received another shove.

"Cool it," Pete growled under his breath. "Thank the man and let's be on our way."

Wes hated being corralled like a head of cattle, but Wes paid the man a hefty percentage to keep him from sticking his foot in his mouth so he might as well shut up.

"Thanks again, Doc. Seriously, I'll consider what you said." *Just not so much.*

Once outside, Wes thought Pete would strangle him. "What's the matter with you? You don't argue with the sponsor."

"I don't take orders from them, either. Besides, he only works for the sponsor."

"And now they know you're injured and you're refusing surgery." Pete pulled a pack of cigarettes out of his pocket and lit one. "If they don't pull your sponsorship now, they sure as hell won't renew it next year." He took a long drag and exhaled slowly. "We're talking a lot of money, Wes. And that's just from one sponsor. I know you don't like the idea of surgery, but Dr. Shelton's right. You get it done now, you're only out for part of the season and next year you'll be as good as new."

Wes snatched the cigarette from his mouth and snapped it in half. "Don't you dare badger me about my well-being while you're blowing smoke in my face."

"You're right, I'm sorry," Pete said sheepishly. "I just feel for you."

"Yeah, well, this is my career we're talking about, not yours. There's no guarantee I'll recover from surgery before next season just like there's no guarantee I'll be able to compete at all. If I wait, I have a shot. I'll get through the pain." Pete opened his mouth to speak, but Wes cut him off before he had a chance. "You can walk back in that arena, snatch up one of the young kids you're so hot to get your hands on and they'll get my sponsorship because I'll be home while they're competing."

"You think I'd be that disloyal to you?"

"No, I think you'd be that smart. You have your own bottom line to watch out for and I can't blame you. I need some time. I need to finish the season and see what happens. I can't even teach after rotator cuff surgery. What am I supposed to do? Ride 'em High! didn't hire me for my good looks."

"Not with your ugly mug." He laughed.

"Do you want me to fire you now or wait till later?"

"Sorry." Pete cleared his throat.

"I need time." If this was his last season, then he needed to make plans. He had to discuss it with his boss in Texas and see what their doctors and physical therapists had to say. More than anything else, he had to keep his head clear and away from all things Jade and the girls.

He'd fly to Montana in the morning, get through Dylan's wedding on Saturday and then fly out that night. Three more days. He'd keep his word and check in on Jade. He'd make sure they had whatever they needed until Liv came home, and then that was it. The girls weren't his to raise and he couldn't get involved with Jade knowing what they'd created and couldn't have. He had to move on. He had too much riding on the next few months and the sooner he got into physical therapy, the better. Nothing had ever interfered with his career and he wasn't about to let anything or anyone start now.

Chapter Seven

Emma and Dylan had been gracious enough to invite Jade to the rehearsal dinner Friday night at the lodge, but she declined. After handing Tomás every key to her queendom along with check-writing capabilities, she was on the verge of a mini-meltdown. She thrived on control, as did Liv. Even though she had promoted Tomás last week, it wasn't the same as giving him access to the business bank accounts to pay vendors and their employees along with the power to make both business and financial decisions in her absence. After a caterer almost bailed because she couldn't transfer funds into their account on time, she realized something had to give.

She trusted Tomás, she just didn't like relying on someone else to run her company or any other aspect of her life. Which must be driving Liv crazy, because that's exactly what Jade was doing for her. She wished her sister would call. They'd never gone this long without some form of communication. Whether it had been a brief text message or a voice mail, they'd kept in contact with each other. Every morning she reached for her phone and fought the disappointment of the deafening silence.

"How about we go for a walk?" Jade asked the girls, who were happily rocking in the new infant seats Wes had bought them. He was right, they really were a godsend. Emma showed her how she used hers with her six-month-old daughter, Holly, who Jade was relieved to see looked nothing like the triplets. Feeding and naps were much easier and she was sure Liv would appreciate that when she returned home.

Jade bundled the girls in their triplet stroller and set off on the paved path that wound around the ranch. "Your mommy would love it here." It was unfortunate Wes and Liv hadn't been a real couple. The girls would have enjoyed growing up on the ranch with family. It was ironic in a way. Liv wanted family so desperately, and even chose a man to father her children from Saddle Ridge's largest, yet they both wanted to keep the girls a secret from their cousins, aunts and uncles. Jade and Liv never had any of those people in their lives. Maybe if they had they would have grown up loved.

Her sister's poor decision making still bothered her. It had been one thing to ask Jade to be the egg donor. But Wes? Lookswise, there was no arguing he was a fine specimen of a man. But his attitude…maybe not so much considering she hadn't seen him since before he left for South Dakota on Tuesday. He'd come back last night, according to Maddie, who had seen him while she was locking lips with Jarrod behind the stables. He texted her and had even called twice, but she had been on the phone with Tomás and a client and couldn't answer. When she called back, it went straight to voice mail, as if he'd turned off his phone.

It didn't matter, anyway. Wes was leaving for good in a few days and so would she once Liv came home. Although she should probably stick around for a month—if not more—afterward to make sure Liv was truly okay alone with the girls. Jade still couldn't quite pocket the anger she had about that. It would be much easier if the four of them came back with her to California. With the exception of her ex-husband, her sister had no other ties to town. She worked remotely and could do the same job from Los Angeles. Jade didn't think it was selfish to point that fact out to both the doctor and Liv. Jade had been more than reasonable so far.

Up ahead in the distance, Jade saw Wes atop a beautiful black-and-white quarter horse giving a group of guests a riding lesson in a large, dirt-covered outdoor arena. *Damn, he looked good.* She checked her watch, surprised he wasn't at the rehearsal dinner. She set the brake on the stroller and crouched down beside the girls. "Look, that's your da— Oh dear!"

I can't believe I almost said daddy. Jade stood up and quickly released the brake. If she could slip up that easily now, what would happen if she made that kind of mistake when the girls were older. As she turned the stroller around, she noticed Wes watching them. Within seconds, he was at the fence and Jade noticed a sling around his neck and arm.

She tried to tell herself she didn't care, but the cold, hard fact was she did. "What happened to you?"

Wes smiled down at the girls who were intently looking up at his horse. "I had a run-in with a bull and dislocated my shoulder. This is just a precaution while it heals."

Jade's palms began to throb from gripping the stroller handle too tight. "I still don't understand all the fuss over eight seconds. It's so dangerous."

His expression hardened. "Those eight seconds require a lot of skill and athleticism."

"Don't get your boxers in a wad." Jade hated when men got touchy about sports. "I'm not saying anything to the contrary. I just don't get the attraction."

"I wear boxer briefs, thank you. I'm not going to lie…there's an adrenaline rush every time I compete. But it's also my job, and those mighty highs are sometimes accompanied by devastating lows." Wes nudged his mount closer to the fence. "Is this the first time they've seen a horse?"

Jade peered over the top of the stroller, trying desperately not to picture Wes wearing nothing but boxer briefs. "They've um—they've seen the Belgians from a distance. I think they may be more fascinated with you though. We—uh—they haven't seen you in a few days."

His mouth curved into a cocky grin. "You're cute when you're flustered."

He shifted in his saddle and Jade wondered if she affected him the same delicious way he affected her. His eyes perused her body before stopping at her breasts. She'd always been self-conscious of their generous size, but Wes's appreciative gaze made every nerve ending in her body prickle with desire. Definitely not thoughts she should be having about the man who defined *complicated*.

A muscle twitched along his jawline as he returned his gaze to hers. "I've been busy helping my family with the upcoming weddings this weekend. I heard you're planning Garrett and Delta's ceremony."

"It's going to be so sweet." Relieved by the subject change, Jade began to relax. "There really wasn't much to it since they stressed simplicity. But it will be uniquely different from Dylan and Emma's wedding."

"I've never seen your face light up so much before." Wes's devastating smile made her bite her bottom lip to prevent her jaw from hitting the ground.

"I love event planning. It brings people together and makes them happy. Speaking of which, why aren't you at the rehearsal dinner?"

"Because the ranch has guests and my brothers have their hands full. I went to the ceremony rehearsal and told Garrett I would take his evening lesson. I thought you'd be there."

"I guess Emma told you she invited me. Is that the real reason you didn't go?"

Wes averted his eyes, giving Jade her answer.

"Well, we'll be seeing you, then." She spun the stroller around and started back to the cabin.

"I told you the truth but that wasn't good enough. You had to dig deeper."

"Go away." Jade waved to him over her shoulder.

"Jade, stop. It's not like that." Wes paced her on his horse. "It's complicated."

"Seriously?" Jade continued down the path. "You're

going to talk to me about complicated when I've uprooted my life more than you have. You get to go home in a few days." Jade stopped herself from adding, *while I'm stuck here*. She didn't want to think of Audra, Hadley and Mackenzie that way despite feeling like a prisoner of sorts.

"At least you still have your career."

"What?" Jade stopped and looked up at him. "What happened?"

"There are a lot of factors involved, but the short of it is, my competing days may be over before my planned retirement and I'm not sure what to do. Chirp on all you want about giving up more than me, but I may have just lost everything." He ran his hand down the horse's neck and gave him a scratch. "This is one of those days I wish Liv was here. She was the best sounding board."

Jade knew she should maintain a friendly distance from Wes, but couldn't fathom having to give up her career. Especially at such a young age. "I realize the girls and I are part of your problem, but if you're willing to join us for dinner, I'm willing to listen. I can't replace her advice, but I'm here."

"You're not a problem, Jade. I'm sorry I ever made you think that." He glanced over his shoulder at the guests. "Where's Maddie tonight?"

"On a date with Jarrod. And Alyssa and Megan are babysitting your brothers' kids." Jade still had work to finish, but she craved adult conversation more. "I wouldn't mind the company."

He nodded. "Give me an hour to finish here and clean up."

"Great." A giddy rush swept over her at the thought of cooking for him. "Do you like Italian?"

"Love it. I'll see you soon." He winked before riding away and she couldn't be sure if it had been at her or the girls. Probably the girls, although she secretly wished otherwise. There were a thousand reasons why she should stay away from Wes Slade, but they had suddenly escaped her brain. And she was okay with that. At least for one night.

"I DIDN'T REALIZE you could cook like that." Stuffed, Wes willed himself to stand and help Jade clear the kitchen table. "It definitely beats the pizza we ordered last week."

Jade had fed the girls before he arrived, giving them time to enjoy their meal. It hadn't been candlelight and champagne, but between her vintage yellow floral dress and the wine, it bordered on romantic to him. He tried to ignore the ever-increasing emotions churning in his gut, drawing him to her like a bear to honey. He was failing. Miserably.

"Chicken scaloppine is one of my specialties. A perk of working with some of LA's finest chefs and caterers is I get to learn how they prepare many of their signature dishes."

"I think I would gain ten pounds a week if I ate your cooking every day." His hand brushed hers as he handed her another plate, causing the hair on his arm to stand on end at the jolt of excitement she sent through him. If this was her effect on him without trying, he'd be a goner if they were an actual couple.

"No, you wouldn't," she said as she rinsed the silverware and dropped it in the dishwasher basket. "Half the time I skip dinner because I've been nibbling throughout the day and the other half of the time I order out because Tomás and I are working an event."

"How is he managing without you?"

"I guess I should say he's doing great. The problem is we're losing clients because I'm not there. He's overworked because he hasn't found a suitable replacement for his old position. It's going to take an extraordinary candidate to do what he does, which is why I told him to hire two people. While he's interviewing, he's also doing a large portion of my job. He has the mentality of 'I'd rather do it myself than delegate it' and he's quickly learning he has to let go of the smaller things. On the flip side, Tomás and the rest of my team have managed to bring in some lucrative last-minute clients like a movie wrap party the other night. Filming finished way ahead of schedule and they needed something large, lavish and fast. With my contacts and Tomás's vision, he pulled off a quarter-of-a-million-dollar party in under twelve hours."

"That's incredible." Wes couldn't imagine wasting that much money on a party. "Then why do you still seem nervous?"

"The company is my baby, my spouse, my everything. The day I graduated, I bought a one-way bus ticket to Los Angeles and the following week I got a job at an event planning company. The job itself sucked. The pay was horrible. But I loved seeing how we took nothing and turned it into something beautiful." Wes may not personally care for frivolous spending, but he enjoyed the way Jade's features grew more animated as she spoke. "At the end of the day, no matter how tired we were, we had something spectacular to show for it. I worked my way up until I was ready to start my own business."

"I didn't realize you left right after high school." Wes had an inclination she'd left because of the misery he'd unknowingly created for her.

"I couldn't get out of this town fast enough. It's not like I had good memories here. That's why I don't understand Liv's attraction to it. If it was all about Kevin, then maybe I can convince her to come back to California with me."

Jade poured two mugs of coffee and handed them to Wes. "Can you bring these into the living room while I move the girls' chairs?"

"Why don't you let me do that?" Wes watched their content faces as Jade lifted the first chair off the dining room floor.

"It's okay, I got it."

Audra and Hadley looked around the room and continued to discover the taste of their own hands, while Mackenzie peacefully snoozed.

"They really love those things, don't they?" Not seeing any coasters, Wes set the hot cups on a parenting magazine on the end table.

"I think I may love them more than they do. I switch the chairs on and once they fall asleep, I put them in their cribs. Usually they're all asleep by now, but you're their favorite shiny new toy. I can't thank you enough. Liv will love them too."

"Shiny new toy, huh?" Wes laughed. "I can't say I've ever been described that way before. All kidding aside, maybe you shouldn't tell Liv they're from me."

"Why? Maddie said she was hurt when you ended your friendship. I would think she'd be happy you gave her this gift."

"Maybe, maybe not. I still wonder if she saw us with the kids that night."

"If she did, she's in the right place to deal with it." Jade shrugged her shoulders. "I don't mean that to sound as harsh as it does. The reality of the situation is, whether she did or didn't is out of our control. I can't keep dwelling on it and neither should you. I'm having a difficult enough time mentally preparing for the pediatrician on Tuesday."

"What's so scary about a pediatrician?"

"I'm afraid if she thinks I'm doing something wrong, they'll take the girls from me. I know it sounds irrational, but I can't shake the thought." Wes noticed a slight tremble in Jade's body as she spoke. "I've read my sister's books at the house, and I think I'm following every parenting blog on the internet, but I have nothing to compare it to. Even Maddie said the same thing. We've never done this before. At least she has a little more experience from helping Liv. Then again, Liv never did it before, either. What if the doctor feels I'm not qualified to care for them? And why are you laughing at me?" She swatted him.

Wes gently cupped her face in his hand. "Because it

doesn't work that way and you're doing an amazing job. Look at them." His hand slid down her shoulder, turning her body away from him. His chest pressed lightly against her back as he eased behind her. The fingers on his good arm lightly trailed down her waist and settled on her hip. "Those are three very blissful babies." He leaned into her, wishing he could pull her even closer and shield her from the pain of the past and erase her fears of tomorrow. "They are healthy, well-nourished children. They're clean. They have clean clothes and a small village of people willing to pitch in. Nobody is going to take them away."

"I want to believe you." Her voice broke as she whispered, "It's so hard."

Wes shifted behind her and lifted his sling over his head.

"Don't you need to wear that?"

"I'm supposed to keep my arm as close to my body as possible. Unless I'm—how did you put it?— bouncing on the back of a bull, I'm not really in any pain without it. The sling just makes me aware of what I shouldn't do with my arm until it heals. I think I can make a small exception."

Wes moved to the corner of the couch, softly tugging her to join him. Wordlessly she settled between his legs, her back still to him. He was pushing the boundaries of their relationship more than he should, but the overwhelming need to protect and care for the four females who'd interrupted and taken over his life won out.

"I know you went through hell growing up. But what your mom did and what you're doing are worlds apart from one another. You're not the same person she was. No one is going to compare you to her."

"Why not? I can't help comparing Liv to my mom." Jade's voice pitched. "I'm disgusted with myself for even thinking it. What if that's what happened to my mom?"

"Your mom was a drug addict." Wes wrapped his arms around her, inadvertently resting on top of her breasts. One lone part of his body twitched at the skin-on-skin contact and he prayed the reaction didn't become too evident.

"Maybe that's why. She got pregnant with me a year after Liv was born. What if she had PPD after me and didn't know how to handle it? I've read numerous reports citing a genetic link to postpartum depression. She said our dad wasn't around. That he was some loser drifter, but he had to have been around for at least two years because Liv and I have the same father. At least that's what she told us."

"Have you ever attempted to contact him?" Wes tried to imagine what life would have been like never knowing his father.

"I can't. Our mom never told us who he was, and we have no idea where she is or if she's still alive. There's no father listed on our birth certificates. I cringed when I had to show it to get my driver's license and passport. The woman at the post office had the nerve to argue with me over the blank field on my passport form. Everyone in line behind me heard me explain I didn't know who my father was. I was so embarrassed. Stuff like that happens, even in this day and age. That's another reason I'm surprised Liv chose the route she did. She hated that growing up."

"By the time the girls are old enough to know what a birth certificate is, I'd like to think people will be more educated to the changing family dynamic."

"I like that you get it." Jade tilted her head and looked up at him. His eyes trailed over her face, stopping on her full red lips. How did her lipstick manage to stay on through dinner? He wanted to kiss her to see if it would survive the heat between them. More than that, he wanted to kiss away her worries and promise her everything would be all right.

"I agreed to be a donor so the fact I accept a modern family shouldn't surprise you."

"Nothing should surprise me at this point, but every time I turn around something else does." Her sultry voice, whether intentional or not, only heightened his desire.

"Like what?" The selfish part of him secretly wished she'd say her attraction to him, while the logical side of him hoped she didn't.

"Like your comment earlier about your career possibly being over."

Wes's heart thudded to a jarring stop. He had managed to forget the realities of his job for the past hour. "A bull rider has a short shelf life as do many other sport professionals. By the time you hit thirty, your body starts feeling every fall three and four times more than you did in your early twenties. Especially when the same injuries keep reoccurring."

"Is that what happened with your shoulder?" Concern etched deep in her features as she frowned up at him.

"Pretty much." Wes rested his head against the back of the couch and stared at the ceiling, not wanting to see the pity he was certain would follow. "Now I need to make the decision to either have surgery and sit out for the next six months, possibly longer, or try to finish this season, then rest for a few months and try it one more time."

"Six months?" Jade twisted sideways, draping her bare legs across his jeans as the hem of her dress rose, exposing her more to him. Her toned thighs begged to be caressed and his inner voice begged to comply. "I can't imagine not being able to work for that long."

Unable to tear his gaze from her body, he allowed himself the pleasure of studying it without physically touching her. He wanted to memorize every inch, every curve. And the woman had curves. Luscious Marilyn Monroe curves that tested the seams of the cotton dress's bodice. The tops of her full breasts rose with each breath. He silently thanked God the zipper was in the back because the urge to set them free quickly became a test of his willpower.

"I'm glad you see it that way." Wes wished he had kept on his sling. It would have given him a place to rest his arm. He lifted it to drape across the back of the couch and winced. Silently he cursed, at the pain and the effect Jade had on him. He patted the cushion next to him, hoping the steady beat would force his heartbeat back on track. "My doctor and my agent don't. It's not just a financial thing. I've made quite a bit competing and I've socked a lot of it away. Not being able to compete means not being able to teach. It also means someone younger can come in and take my place both in the arena and at the rodeo school. Big names attract spectators, sponsors and students."

"Humor me for a second and allow me to play devil's advocate. If you are planning to retire at the end of next season, what is so bad about retiring this year?"

"For starters, I wanted to retire on my own terms. To go out on top, with another championship win. I haven't had one since I was twenty-six. I've been chasing my own success for three years. If I retire with the championship, I'll have more options afterward."

"What kind of options?"

"Endorsement deals and collaborations with equipment manufacturers, my own bull riding clinics, TV analyst gigs." Everything his father said he could be if he worked hard enough. The man may have questioned teenage rumors and have been cruel with his words at times, but he believed in Wes's ability to win. "There are a lot of options when you're one of the best. And I was one of the best. And then I made mistakes."

"Mistakes as in your agreement with Liv?"

"If you had asked me that question a few weeks ago I would've answered yes." Wes still couldn't believe how attached he'd grown to the girls in a little over a week. "Liv, my uncle's death, moving to Texas and their birth…they were all distractions. But no, helping to bring Audra, Hadley and Mackenzie into this world definitely wasn't a mistake. Even with all the past issues between us and your sister's postpartum depression, I'm glad I did it. I just want them to grow up happy."

Jade laid her head on his shoulder as they watched the three beautiful lives they'd unknowingly created together. "So this is what normal feels like."

Wes started to laugh. "I'm not sure if I'd call our arrangement normal."

"No, I mean two adults at home on the couch while the little ones drift off to sleep. The closest I've ever gotten to the experience is on a TV show. It's nice."

"Yeah, it is." Wes buried his nose in her hair, never wanting to forget the scent of her shampoo. Contentment washed over him as he held her while watching their daughters. It was wrong for him to think of them that way, but he wanted that pleasure. Just for one night. He'd never be this close to having a family ever again. And that was okay, because this was the only family he wanted to remember. That realization welled in his chest. He didn't want to be a dad. He didn't want a wife or a family. His career and livelihood were collapsing around him and all he wanted to do was stay in this moment and not let go.

Chapter Eight

Jade hated to miss a wedding or any party, for that matter. It went against every fiber of her being. More important, she hated not being able to see Wes amongst
the groomsmen. She even bet he'd be the most handsome man there. The more time she spent with him,
the more she liked him beyond the physical attraction.
If they had reconnected for any other reason, they may
have had a fighting chance at something real.

A cool Montana summer breeze fluttered the cur-
tains on the open windows. It was perfect outdoor wedding weather and the forecasted clear night would make
for a magical reception under a star-filled sky.

Technically she could attend the wedding. Emma had
extended her an invite but, despite receiving many of-
fers to babysit the triplets, Jade felt it was more important for the bride and groom's friends to attend instead
of her. She just wished the ceremony wasn't happening
on the most remote part of the ranch where she couldn't
even catch a glimpse of it.

Jade stepped onto the porch. It was still surreal to
her to walk out a front door and see wide-open spaces.

Even when she lived in Saddle Ridge as a kid, there had always been other houses surrounding them.

The ranch was quiet this afternoon. At least where the cabin was. She envisioned the bustle of the bride and her attendants as she got ready, and the guests filing into the newly constructed wedding venue overlooking town and the Swan Range. Jarrod had picked up Maddie an hour ago, giving her a chance to give her friend her seal of approval. She'd spent fifteen minutes with them and she could already envision their wedding.

Jade had developed a sixth sense about relationship longevity years ago and she had a pretty good track record at picking the odds. She could also tell when her own relationships were doomed and had learned to eliminate the heartbreak by getting out early on. The problem with Wes was, if she removed Liv and the girls from the equation, she didn't see that heartbreak potential. She genuinely liked him and wanted to spend whatever time they had left together. But her sister and the triplets did exist and no amount of justification would make any relationship with Wes right.

It wasn't fair. She'd made a career of planning happily-ever-afters and her life was more of a lonely-ever-after. Los Angeles was the land of opportunity. Where big dreams were made and realized. For the most part, Jade lived that life and she'd been satisfied. Now that she'd had a taste of family, she wanted it. Only the family she wanted wasn't hers to keep.

Jade stormed back inside, annoyed for worrying about her love life instead of Liv's recovery. She wasn't in Montana for herself. She was there for her sister and no sacrifice should be too big. Then why did it already feel like it was?

"It's all temporary, Jade," she said to no one as she pulled out a kitchen chair and sat at the large round table covered in wedding paraphernalia. Any feelings she had for Wes were only in the here and now. In a few months, they would be a distant memory. She shook her head to clear him from her brain. "Okay…time to focus on Delta and Garrett's wedding tomorrow."

Jade checked and rechecked her lists. Even though the sunrise ceremony was much more casual than tonight's wedding, there was still a lot involved to pull it together before the guests arrived. Normally she'd schedule vendors to come in and do all the setup, but Delta and Garrett's budget left Jade doing much of the work herself. It had been a long time since she'd planned an old-school wedding, and she secretly loved every minute of it. Even with teams of people helping her back home, the intense stress to coordinate every event was exhausting. This wasn't. From assembling table centerpieces in mason jars, hand folding silverware napkin pouches and arranging a bridal bouquet from flowers grown on the ranch, Jade welcomed this new level of stress. She enjoyed her celebrity events in Los Angeles, but she loved the close family atmosphere of this more.

It's only temporary.

"Go away." Jade didn't need her inner voice reminding her none of it was hers to keep.

"How did you even know I was here?" a man said from the doorway. "I haven't knocked yet."

"Wes!" Jade shot out of her chair so fast she almost

knocked it over. "You scared me half to death." She quickly grabbed the baby monitor to see if she woke the girls. "What are you doing here?"

Good heavens! Jade gripped the table for support. Wes's tall silhouette in the open door frame was a memory she never wanted to forget. His broad shoulders, lean waist and muscular long legs made her breath catch in her throat. But it was when he took a step forward and she saw him standing before her in his black cowboy hat, dress Wranglers and boots, white button-down shirt and silver-gray vest that her tummy flip-flopped a thousand times over.

"You look great." Had she just said that out loud? *Get control, girl.*

"Thank you." He touched the brim of his hat and nodded.

Now, that was something she didn't see in LA. "What are you doing here and where's your sling?"

"I refuse to wear that thing today. I'll be fine if I don't overuse my shoulder or arm. And I'm here to escort you to the wedding."

"Did Emma or Maddie put you up to this?"

"Nobody puts me up to anything. Emma would like you to be there, though. Megan's mom is on her way over to babysit the girls and before you argue with me, she said she's happy to do it."

"I appreciate the offer, but I need to work on tomorrow's wedding. I have to start setting up as soon as the reception ends tonight. Delta and Garrett put together a group of volunteers for me."

"I know. I'm one of the volunteers."

"You?" Jade mentally kicked herself for not realizing Garrett would ask him for help. It was a given. Yet in the back of her mind, she couldn't wait to see Wes's appreciation for her contribution to his brother's wedding. Especially since she refused to accept any payment beyond the necessary supply and rental fees. This was her gift to Delta for being such a good friend to her sister. She would have preferred to cover all the expenses, but the bride and groom refused.

Wes crossed the room to her. "I won't take no for an answer." He placed both hands on her shoulders and turned her toward the hallway. "By the time you're ready, the sitter will be here. Just don't take too long, I have to be there in twenty minutes."

"Twenty minutes?" Jade tried to look at him over her shoulder as he continued to push her toward the bedroom. "Nothing like giving a girl short notice." Truth was, Jade had mastered the art of getting ready for a formal event in under ten minutes. It was a requirement in her industry, especially on the occasion she juggled multiple events in one day.

"I will spend the rest of the night helping you with whatever you need." He stopped and released her shoulders as they reached the girls' bedroom.

"Wes?" Jade whispered. The smile he'd worn only moments ago had faded to sadness. "What is it?"

"In twenty-four hours, I'll be on a plane to Texas. I'll never see them again."

Jade rested her hand lightly on his arm, uncertain how to console him. She couldn't even begin to comprehend the thought of walking away forever.

"Liv's original plan may have been to keep you out of their lives, but she may not feel that way now. There's still hope."

"That's a big if, and until I know for sure, I can't allow myself that hope. I made an agreement with your sister and I have to stand by that unless she says otherwise. I can't just watch from a distance, though. You should go get ready," Wes said before walking back to the dining area.

Jade didn't know which was harder...remaining in their lives and always wondering what could've been, or never having the opportunity to see them grow up. Either choice was a tremendous sacrifice and there was no alternative.

She sealed herself in her room and leaned against the door. The realization she may never see Wes again struck her heart like a lightning bolt splits an oak. Attending the wedding with him would be the only *date* they'd ever have. Not that dating Wes was ever a possibility. Then why did it hurt?

She quickly tugged her shirt over her head with one hand while opening the closet door with the other. She'd found the sweetest vintage clothing store in town the day she met with Liv's attorney. The shop owner had been setting out a display of '50s dresses and other outfits, all in her size. They'd fit as if they had been made for her and Jade couldn't resist buying the whole collection.

She removed a red-and-white rose dress from the hanger and slipped it on. The tailored bodice, nipped waist and full, flared skirt accentuated her curves and made her waist appear smaller. And she was all for anything that thinned her out a bit. The accompanying petticoat added a touch of extra volume and made her feel ultrafeminine and a little giddy about attending the wedding with Wes. Of course, he would be up front with his brothers during the ceremony, but a small part of her looked forward to a dance afterward. Jade hadn't allowed herself that pleasure in years because it was a rarity she was a guest at anything. Tonight, she'd make an exception. It was the last chance she'd have to enjoy Wes's company on a personal level and she wanted to savor it, because come tomorrow night, she'd miss him and what could never be. Tonight was theirs.

WES STRUTTED PROUDER than a peacock down the white pine walkway of the wedding venue with Jade on his arm. He heard a few gasps, a hint of a whisper here and there and quite a few "they look lovely together" from the older crowd as they made their way to the front of the outdoor ceremony site.

Dylan had designed and built the gazebo and sur-rounding venue seating as a wedding gift for Emma on the very spot they had fallen in love. It had been six months of hard labor to complete it on time, but the location overlooking Saddle Ridge with the majestic Swan Range before them was their declaration of love to one another in front of everyone and heaven above.

For a man who'd never cared about sentiment or long-term relationships, these past two weeks at home had forever altered Wes's sense of family. He wanted someone to look at him the way Emma looked at his brother. He wanted someone to plan the rest of his life with and children to watch grow up and raise families of their own. He wanted the woman who was ever so slightly pressed against him. The woman whose perfume tickled his nose in an "I can't get enough" kind of way. He wanted the chance to see where things could lead with Jade. Even an early retirement didn't look so bad with her in the picture. Only she wasn't in the picture. At least not past tomorrow.

Wes clenched his fist against the painful vise slowly squeezing the life out of his heart. Twenty-three hours and counting before he stepped on that plane. It would be all right once he was away from Jade and the girls. It had to be because he couldn't live with the agony of always wondering *what if.* He just needed some time to shake it off. And since he refused to retire early, he needed to focus all his attention on winning the championship.

"I'm so glad you decided to join us." Dylan hugged Jade. "Emma will be too."

"You did a beautiful job." Jade glanced around at the long, curved pine benches Dylan had permanently built into the ground. "It's absolutely breathtaking here. I never knew Saddle Ridge could be so beautiful."

Neither could Wes.

"Emma and I hope to one day see our children get married here. And maybe the rest of both our families will choose this place too." Dylan nudged Wes. "You're next, little bro."

"Yeah, that's not going to happen," Wes said, feeling as if his tie was suddenly about to choke him to death.

As he adjusted it, he noticed Jade's shoulders sag as she turned away from him. *Crap!* Even though they both knew they had zero chance of a future together, he could've chosen his words a little more carefully. He looked up at Dylan, who stood there shaking his head. *Double crap!* "Why don't I show you to your seat?"

"I can manage, thank you." Jade hurried to her seat before he had a chance to stop her. He would've appreciated a private second alone to explain himself, although what explanation was needed? Neither one of them could possibly be that disillusioned to believe they had anything past tomorrow.

"Go after her." Dylan gave him a friendly shove.

"No." Wes took his place beside his brother. "It's not like that between us. We're just friends."

"I don't know who you're trying to convince, but there's a lot more between you and Jade than friendship."

"Are you ready?" Reverend Grady asked Dylan. "I just got word your bride is on her way."

"I've never been more ready." Dylan excitedly rubbed his hands together.

Garrett squeezed in between them. "Let's get you married."

Once again, neither of his brothers had chosen him to be best man at their weddings. It was such a petty thing, but considering they had been each other's best man at their first weddings, it would have been nice if they could have chosen him and Harlan to stand up for them this time around.

Harlan clapped him on the back. "Hey," he whispered. "The other day Belle and I decided to renew our vows and I want you to be my best man. I didn't have one last year and I'd really like you to do the honors."

Leave it to Harlan to pick up on his insecurities. "Are you sure you don't want to ask one of them?"

"Nope. I choose you and you better be there. August 1, no excuses. We're going to have a real wedding this time. Maybe Jade will still be here since it's only five weeks away."

"Not you, too." Wes smoothed the front of his vest as a white, antique horse-drawn carriage crested the horizon. "Jade and I can never be more than friends."

"Who knows, maybe she'll move here." Garrett chimed in on his right.

Wes tugged at the collar of his shirt. "She has a lucrative business in LA and I have no intentions of ever going Hollywood."

"She isn't going to want him after what he said earlier," Dylan added. "Poor guy doesn't know what he's missing." His smile widened as Delta's father helped her down from the coach. "Love, marriage, kids…it's everything."

"It sure is," his other two brothers said in unison before Harlan leaned over and whispered, "What did you say to Jade earlier?"

"Shh." Wes brushed him off. Getting ganged up on by his siblings was the last thing he needed. Especially with Jade watching him from three rows away.

She looked beautiful today and he hadn't even had the decency to tell her. Her retro glam made his heart race every time. A part of him longed to go back in time to the decade she wore so well. Where life was simpler and modern science didn't complicate matters. If they had been a couple, they wouldn't have had Hadley, Mackenzie and Audra at the same time, but Wes was a firm believer in destiny and the girls would've been born regardless. Of course, all the stars would have had to align in order for them to be together today.

Emma's best friend led Garrett's children down the aisle, followed by Belle and Delta pushing Travis and Holly in white strollers ahead of the bride. Every member of his family—both blood and extended—were a part of Dylan and Emma's wedding. Everyone except Audra, Hadley and Mackenzie. They could have been right beside their cousins in their own strollers and included in all the wedding photos the family would pose for later. Photos that would hang on walls for decades to come and grace the pages of albums for future generations to look through.

Liv had wanted a family, but in creating that family, the three of them had collectively and knowingly excluded the girls from their *true* family. That had always been the plan. Wes had never wanted anyone to know he'd fathered his best friend's children. Now that plan seemed so shortsighted.

At the time, he'd only factored in his own feelings and hadn't considered the bigger picture. That's not to say he would have changed his mind and done things any differently. But maybe, just maybe, he would've come up with a solution that included his family in the girls' lives. He was powerless to change the situation now. He'd made his decision a year ago and was legally bound to it. The law may prevent him from calling them his girls, but in his heart, they would forever be *his girls*. And Jade would always be the mother of his children.

"Friends, family and neighbors," Reverend Grady began. "We are gathered here today to celebrate the union of Dylan Slade and Emma Sheridan. Over the past year, I've come to know the Slade family rather well. I've officiated over two of their weddings, two christenings and sadly one funeral. During that time, I've noticed one common thread interwoven throughout this family. The thread of love."

Love. All four of his brothers had fallen in love and had been married at least once. Three of those marriages had ended in devastating heartbreak. Love and heartbreak were two concepts that had eluded him for twenty-nine years. It was impossible to get your heart broken if you didn't fall in love. Yet somehow, in a few short weeks he'd learned the meaning of both words. The love he had for his daughters was like nothing he'd ever experienced before. And tomorrow he'd experience heartbreak for the first time when he walked away.

JADE SENSED WES'S unease during the ceremony and she wondered if the same thing she'd been thinking ran through his head, as well. That a massive family celebration was missing three new members. She couldn't help questioning her sister's logic once again. She understood Liv's desire to personally know her children's father, but why Wes? Why did she choose the man with the largest family in town? And why did she choose the one man Jade couldn't get out of her head.

She'd only been around him for a week and a half and she found herself tempted by the forbidden fruit. Her sister had spent almost five years with him. Their friendship had lasted longer than Liv's marriage. Despite Wes believing Liv was still in love with Kevin, she couldn't picture her sister pining for anyone that long. They hadn't even missed their mom for more than a few months and she was the only family they had outside of each other.

As the reception began, Jade attempted to slip away unnoticed. The ceremony itself was the most important part of a wedding, although she hoped no one ever told her bridal clients that. The money was in the after party.

"Excuse me." A woman lightly tapped her shoulder. "Are you Jade Scott?"

Jade turned to see Molly Weaver, Harlan's ex-wife. "Wow, I wasn't expecting to see you here." The last she had heard, Molly had left town shortly after her divorce.

"I moved back to town last year. I'm sorry to hear about your sister."

Jade's hackles rose. "Um, okay what did you hear about Liv?"

Molly paled. "Oh, maybe Harlan shouldn't have told me."

Nice. Real nice. Wes had assured her that his family wouldn't broadcast Liv's illness around town and his brother had done just that. "Liv is a fighter and this time away will only make her stronger. She'll be back before we know it."

"I'm sure she will. And just so you know, the only reason Harlan told me is because I walked out on my daughter when she was only a year old. He asked me the other day if I'd felt the same despair postpartum depression women experience."

"Did you?"

"Possibly. It was seven years ago and I was very overwhelmed by the prospect of being a parent. My pregnancy wasn't planned like your sister's was. It happened, and nine months later I found myself married to a man I didn't love with a daughter I wasn't sure what to do with. And I tried. I did. But walking away was easier than trying harder. It took me six years to figure that out. Even if PPD had been a factor in the beginning, the rest was all on me and my selfishness."

"Why are you telling me this?"

"Because regardless of why you leave your children for someone else to raise, that guilt stays with you. Even after you do the right thing whether that be returning or staying away—and I firmly believe some parents should stay away—the guilt never leaves. I just wanted you to be aware of that when your sister eventually comes home. She'll have to live with that for the rest of her life. You'll understand that bond one day when you have children of your own."

Jade's stomach knotted. "I appreciate your candor. What is your relationship like now with your daughter?"

"We're still navigating the waters. I don't know if she'll ever forgive me completely. I've always heard kids are resilient, and they are to a certain extent. But you never forget your mother walking out on you."

"Oh, believe me, my sister and I understand that all too well."

Molly's hands flew to her mouth. "Jade, I'm so sorry. I totally forgot you and Liv had been orphaned."

Orphaned. The word irked her. Orphaned meant the child hadn't had a choice in their fate. Both Liv and Jade had decidedly concluded they were better off without their mother and had said as much in court. "No worries. Our mother didn't exactly walk out on us, she walked out on herself."

"I didn't mean to bring up any bad memories. I guess I just wanted to say I'm here if you want to talk. Maybe I can give you some perspective from the other side. Again, my situation differed from your sister's, but I'm sure a lot of the sentiment is the same." Molly looked past Jade. "I think someone wants your attention."

Jade turned around to see Wes walking toward them. So much for her slipping away unnoticed.

"Molly," Wes said through gritted teeth.

"Hi, Wes. I'll leave you two alone. Think about what I said."

"I will. Thank you."

"What did she want?" Wes asked as Molly walked away.

"She heard about Liv and said she could sympathize. She really has changed since high school. She's trying, Wes. If Harlan can give her a second chance, you can too."

His brow furrowed. "She really did a number on my niece and brother."

"And forgiveness is hard-won, but sometimes when you look deep within your heart, you realize you've already done it."

Wes's jaw hung slack. "Are you saying what I think you're saying?"

Jade exhaled slowly, relieved to finally release the last of her resentment. "I have forgiven you for the past."

"That means the world to me to hear you say that."

"Now, if you'll excuse me, I need to get back to work." Jade turned away, not wanting to spend any more time around Wes than necessary. While there was no denying his physical attraction to her, his earlier comment to his brother before the ceremony served as a not-so-subtle reminder they could never be anything more than what they were.

"Please don't leave." He touched her arm, sending an instant shiver through her body. "The reception is just starting."

"I have a lot to do for tomorrow."

"No, you don't. While you were getting dressed, I saw your numerous lists on the table and everything was checked off."

"Your brazenness aside, I have other lists for tomorrow morning I still haven't touched on top of the events I'm working on in LA."

"I told you I would help." Wes jammed his hands into his pockets. "This is not going how I planned. Let me start over and begin by apologizing for the way I acted earlier. I was also hoping you would sit with me and my family for the reception. You already know everyone."

"Thank you for the apology, but it isn't necessary. I know where we stand. And I appreciate your offer to help, but the only thing I'll need from you and the others is some assistance setting things up in the morning.

Megan and Alyssa are coming over after the reception and spending the night. They'll help with whatever little things I have left."

"What about Maddie?"

"Since she's Delta's maid of honor, she decided to stay with the rest of the wedding party at the main lodge." Jade doubted anyone would sleep tonight with all the excitement of two weddings. "Could you meet me here at three sharp? That will give us three hours before the ceremony begins."

"Of course." Disappointment registered across his face and Jade wasn't sure if it was because she asked him to meet her at the ungodly hour or if he'd hoped to go back to her place after the wedding. "If you plan on going all night long, you'll need to eat. You're already here and the lodge chefs have prepared an amazing menu. I snuck a taste of a few things this afternoon. Besides, you look amazing in that dress and it would be a shame if people didn't see you wearing it a little longer."

Jade couldn't help herself from smiling at the compliment. "By 'people,' do you mean you?"

"Yes." The stubborn set of his chin told her there was no getting out of dinner. "Shall we?"

Wes offered his arm and for the second time that night, she allowed him to lead her through the maze of familiar faces she hadn't seen since high school. Friends, not-so-friends, store owners and even a teacher or two. She'd known the entire town would be there, but she hadn't taken the time to process who all that would entail. After the thirtieth "it's been so long" over dinner, Jade began to enjoy catching up with people and hearing what they'd done with their lives. She'd even met the woman who'd originally owned the dress she wore and other outfits she'd bought at the vintage store. For the first time, she felt comfortable in Saddle Ridge. The bright lights of LA seemed so far in her past she almost couldn't imagine going back.

Midconversation with her old English teacher, Wes's palm settled on the small of her back. She leaned into the intimate gesture, luxuriating in the heat emanating from his body. Inhaling deeply, she allowed herself the pleasure of his touch. They'd never see each other again after tomorrow and she didn't want to deprive herself of their last moments together.

"Dance with me," he whispered.

His velvet-edged voice against her cheek sent a shiver of excitement straight to her core. Powerless to refuse him, she smiled at her former teacher. "Please excuse me."

Wes gathered her in his arms and elegantly guided her to the dance floor like a seasoned professional. She knew the man had mad skills in the rodeo arena, but she'd never expected him to know how to waltz.

"Are you enjoying yourself?" he asked. His hold firmed as his muscular chest flattened against her breasts and the length of his growing arousal pressed against her belly.

"Immensely," she purred, not meaning the word to sound as sultry as it had. "Are you?"

Wes twisted his face indecisively. "There's just one thing that can make this night better than it already is."

Without waiting for her to respond, he lowered his

mouth to hers, branding her with his lips. His embrace tightened as her trembling limbs clung to him. His kiss, surprisingly gentle yet dangerously erotic, intensified with each stroke of his tongue. Her heart drummed against his chest in unison with his as the rest of the wedding guests slipped away. She had never wanted a man as much as she desired Wes. The ache so great it bordered on unbearable. The man she'd once despised shared a bond with her no one could ever break. In the safety of his arms, nothing could hurt her. If only it could last.

Jade broke their kiss and looked up at him. "We can't do this."

"Yes, we can." Wes dipped his head again and kissed the side of her neck.

She flattened her palms against his chest. "Wes, we are not alone. And I won't be alone all night."

Wes tilted his head back in frustration and groaned. He widened his stance to lower his height closer to hers and held her face between his hands. "Then allow me one more kiss before we say good-night."

His lips claimed hers once more. His kiss, surprisingly soft yet commanding, melted away what remained of her defenses. For once in her life, Jade wished she could hold time in the palm of her hand so this moment would never end.

Chapter Nine

Sleep had alluded Wes in the handful of hours between their kiss and sunrise. A sense of renewed hope grew inside him as he once again stood alongside his brothers in front of their friends and family. He was leaving for the airport in less than twelve hours, and even though he'd sworn never to return to Saddle Ridge, he now looked forward to Harlan's recommitment ceremony in August. A part of him had even considered flying out to visit Jade in Los Angeles. He'd never been fond of the city before, but spending more time with her would be worth the sacrifice. And who knew? Maybe nothing would come out of it, but he wasn't ready to walk away without trying.

Just as the ceremony began, Jade removed her phone from her pocket and quickly walked toward the catering tent. Instinct told him it was about Liv or the girls. He couldn't see her walking away from the wedding she'd meticulously planned for any other reason.

"Do you, Garrett, take Delta to be your lawfully wedded wife, for better or for worse, for richer or for poorer, in sickness and in health, to love and to cherish, forsaking all others from this day forward?"

Wes wanted to follow her, but he couldn't leave mid-ceremony. His insides twisted as a million thoughts ran through his mind. If the call had been about the girls, she would've run. She didn't run. It had to be about Liv. Maybe it was Liv.

"What is wrong with you?" Harlan whispered between clenched teeth beside him.

"Do you, Delta, take Garrett…" Reverend Grady's voice began to sound like the teacher on the *Peanuts* cartoon.

A trickle of sweat ran down his temple as Jade emerged from the tent and quickly made her way back to the ceremony. Her face tight and unreadable. Once seated, he fully expected her to look his way, but she remained focused on Delta and Garrett…as he should be.

"You may now kiss the bride."

The applause and celebratory shouts almost knocked him off balance. The ceremony was over and he'd missed a good part of it. Could he have been any more of an ass? He joined his brothers as they congratulated the couple, fighting the pain that rocketed through him when he gave them a hug. He'd pushed his shoulder to the limit last night on the dance floor with Jade and this morning when they were setting up for the breakfast reception. He was scheduled to compete in Oklahoma later in the week and he seriously doubted he'd be able to.

"Are you okay?" Harlan asked.

"My shoulder's really bothering me." Wes searched

the faces in the crowd for Jade, but he didn't see her. "Excuse me."

Wes jumped off the side of the gazebo and beelined for the catering tent, almost running into Jade as he entered. "Was that call about Liv or the girls?"

"It was Liv's treatment center." Jade looked past him to the wedding guests before returning her attention to him. "It's less than an hour from here." Jade laughed sarcastically. "At the very first place I contacted. Actually, I contacted them a few times but my sister didn't feel the need to let me know where she was."

"Why did they call today? Especially so early."

"Sunday is family day, and Liv wants to see the girls." Jade's features clouded in a mix of joy and sadness. "I have to leave in a few minutes. They would like me to be there by eight so Liv can spend the day with them. Something about an assessment, cognitive therapy and reacclimation sessions. I didn't understand it all, but I'm sure I will once I get there."

"Okay, I'll go with you." Wes reached in his pocket for his phone realizing he'd left it in his cabin. "Let me borrow your phone so I can change my flight."

"What? No." Jade shook her head and walked away from him, checking each of the chafing dish burners. "You need to go home."

"I want to be there when you tell her about us."

Jade shushed him and tugged him to the corner of the tent away from the servers. "I'm not going to ambush my sister by telling her I know you're the girls' father, or that we've been playing house while…"

"While what? Falling for each other? After that kiss, you can't deny there's something between us."

"I can't devastate my sister like that. I don't want her to feel like it's two against one, especially when the two are her daughters' biological parents. I refuse to put her through any unnecessary hell. You need to get on that plane today, and return to your normal routine. Once things settle down, I will talk to her about allowing you to have a relationship with the girls. But this thing between you and me—" Jade swiped at a lone tear rolling down her cheek "—was temporary. We both knew that."

Wes wanted to argue. He wanted to tell her they still had each other, but he knew any involvement with Jade would be a constant reminder of their daughters. He didn't fit into their lives. He was never meant to. He didn't know how to walk away, either.

"Saying goodbye is harder than I thought it would be." He lifted her chin to him. "At least let me come back to the house with you to see the girls one last time." A tightness grew in his chest. "Please give me that much."

"What about the reception?" Jade peered around him. "They're headed this way now. This will be over in an hour, maybe two. A lot of people are traveling home today. You need to be here for your family."

"I need to say goodbye to my daughters," Wes demanded.

"Shh." Jade swatted him. "Keep your voice down."

"You involved me in their lives and as much as I fought against it, they grabbed hold of my heart. I refuse to leave here without saying goodbye, with or without you."

"Okay." Jade rested her hand on his chest. "I'm not trying to hurt you. I thought I would spare you the pain, but I understand your need to see them. Meet me at the cabin. I need to tell Delta and Garrett I'm leaving."

"Tell them I'll be back in a few." Wes stormed out the tent's back flap. He wanted time to say goodbye to the girls...alone. He jerked off his tie as he half walked, half ran to his truck. Safely in the confines of the cab, he smacked the steering wheel. Hard. He didn't know how to do this.

Within minutes he parked beside the cabin. Tugging his wallet from the pocket of his jeans, he removed a couple hundred-dollar bills. He had no idea if Jade had promised Megan and Alyssa more or less, but this would have to do for now. He needed them to leave.

He hopped down from the truck and took the porch stairs two at a time, startling the teens when he opened the screen door. "There's been a little change of plans." Wes held out a folded bill to each of them, his eyes settling on the three cherub faces happily rocking in their chairs. "I will settle up with you later if you're owed any more than that."

"Are you sure?" Megan asked. "We're supposed to stay until the wedding is over."

"I'm sure. In fact, why don't you go down to the reception and have breakfast with everyone else. Jade's on her way here, so I have it covered."

Wes tried to stop fidgeting as he waited for the teens to gather their overnight bags and leave. He only had a few minutes left to spend with the girls. He closed the front door behind them and sat cross-legged on the floor in front of his daughters. Unable to hold back his tears any longer, he lifted Hadley into his arms and cradled her against his chest.

"What have you done to me, little one?" He kissed the top of her head, inhaling her familiar baby scent. "I never meant to fall in love with you, but I couldn't help myself." He brushed the back of his fingers against Mackenzie's cheek as her big sparkling blue eyes met his. "I have to go away for a little while, but I'll be back in August. I don't know if you'll still be here or not, so I have to say goodbye now." Wes heaved a sob. "Oh God, how do I do this? You three will always be a part of me. And I will always watch over you. I promise. You won't know it, but I'll be there. You are my three little gifts from heaven and I will love you forever."

Wes heard the sound of a car door outside the living room window. It wasn't enough time. He wanted more. He needed more. He settled Hadley back in her chair. "You're going to see your mommy today. And she loves you more than life itself." He leaned forward and kissed Audra on the head. "You'll grow up and rule the world. You can be whoever you want to be." Wes wiped at his eyes. "I love you, now and forever."

The front door opened behind him. How could his time be over already? It wasn't fair. He kissed Mackenzie on the forehead and rose, his back to Jade. "Will you call me later and tell me what happened with Liv?"

"Of course," she said softly. "And you can call me whenever you want."

"Yeah, not like that won't be too difficult." Wes reached for his phone to take a picture of them, but he realized he must have left it in his cabin and cursed. "I never got to take one photo of them. Not one. I have nothing to take with me."

"I'll send you all the photos you want." Jade's voice broke.

"No." He shook his head, incapable of saying anything more. He closed his eyes and turned away from the girls, his heart shattering into a million pieces. He forced himself to walk to the door, unable to look back. "Goodbye, Jade."

Wes stepped onto the porch, forever a changed man. A broken man. All the things he'd thought meant something in his life were inconsequential compared to the love for a child…and a woman. His life would never be the same.

A COUNSELOR NAMED Millie carried Audra's car seat down the hall of the postpartum depression treatment center as Jade followed with Hadley and Mackenzie. "This is where most of Liv's initial reacclimation to her daughters will occur." Millie opened the door to a casual living room–type area and held it for Jade to enter. "The visits will increase, and at some point the children will join Liv here at the center so she can learn how to balance her emotions while caring for them."

"Wait, what? I haven't agreed to overnight visits here." Jade set Hadley's and Mackenzie's car seats on the beige carpeted floor. The place may resemble a warm and cozy guest lodge from the outside, but the fact remained it was a treatment facility and she did not feel comfortable leaving the children in a place where women didn't have complete control of their emotions. "I have guardianship and that's not going to happen unless I say so."

Millie's brows arched as she lowered Audra's car seat next to her sisters. "It's part of her treatment plan. Don't you want your sister to improve?"

"I find that question rather insulting." Jade folded her arms across her chest, annoyed she was put on the defensive so soon after arriving. "Of course I want my sister to get better, but unless I'm a hundred percent comfortable with the girls' safety here, they will not stay overnight. Honestly, I find this conversation premature. I haven't even spoken with my sister or her physician yet. I didn't even know where she was until this morning."

Millie calmly clasped her hands in front of her. "I apologize. I was not aware of that. Dr. Stewart will be in shortly to speak with you. Until then, do you have any questions?"

Only a million. "How is my sister?"

"Olivia is relaxed and learning new coping skills. Her situation is more unique than most of our patients because her children aren't biologically hers."

"Liv. No one calls her Olivia." Millie's ultracalm demeanor irked her. "Relaxed as in medicated or relaxed as in Zen?"

"Your sister is not medicated. She had the option and she refused, as do many of our patients. Since she is a single parent, it was important to her to not have to rely on medication or worry about its side effects."

A tall middle-aged woman with silvery hair entered the room. "Hello, Jade. I'm Dr. Stewart. It's a pleasure to meet you." She shook her hand before directing her attention to the girls. "And this must be Mackenzie, Hadley and Audra." She crouched in front of them. "I've heard so much about you."

"I wish I knew more about you and this place." Jade swore every emotion known to man coursed through her body. She hadn't even had time to process Wes's goodbye, before having to run out the door with the girls. She'd known he was leaving today, she just hadn't expected it to be so early or so abrupt. Her phone rang in her bag, wrenching her away from this morning's heartbreak. "I'm sorry. I forgot to mute the ringer on the way in."

"That's fine, just understand this is a phone-free zone," Dr. Stewart warned.

"Of course." Jade silenced her phone, but not before seeing Tomás's name on the screen. He'd have to wait.

After a detailed explanation of the treatment center's protocols and a tour of the ten-acre campus and private grounds, Jade felt more confident her sister had chosen the right place. It was well secured and they even had small cottages with nurseries for the women. By the time they made it back to the visitation room, Jade bore a tinge of remorse for jumping all over Millie earlier.

"Keep in mind, all visits are monitored. We don't want you to hold back your feelings, but we do need you to listen to Liv's feelings. PPD patients have difficulty expressing their emotions, especially when they are overwhelmed. Some exhibit anger while others retreat into themselves. If at any time we believe Liv is struggling, we will step in and guide you both through the process."

"Um, there are a few things I need to tell Liv about the father of her children." Jade had debated having this conversation today during the entire ride there. She relented, rationalizing the more they knew up front, the better they could help her sister. "The thing is, I accidently discovered who the father is and, when Liv had disappeared without a trace, I contacted him in hopes he might know where she went."

Dr. Stewart's eyes widened. "I was under the impression she used an anonymous donor. How did you know where to reach this man?"

"I thought she used an anonymous donor too. When I found out who it was, I was shocked because not only did I go to school with him, his siblings live in town and they have children the girls' age. As they get older, they'll have daily contact with their cousins and not realize it."

Dr. Stewart rubbed the back of her neck and stared at the floor in silence while Millie sat perched on the edge of her chair gaping at her.

Okay. Now what?

"And m-maybe I should also tell you that Wes— that's his name—and his family have been helping me with the girls."

"Helping you?" Dr. Stewart cleared her throat. "So they're aware of their relation to the children."

"Only Wes is. But he left to go home to Texas today. He moved there in January." Jade took a deep breath and recounted the past two weeks in detail to Dr. Stewart and Millie. "We had agreed to tell Liv everything, but I didn't think doing it today was a good idea."

"I can't force you to tell her today, but in my opinion, it's better for her to hear everything now so she can process her feelings. I'd rather have her upset here, early on in her treatment, instead of down the road where she might suffer a setback, accuse you of keeping things from her, or both."

"I wasn't prepared for this today." Jade wrung her hands.

"Like we say here, you can't prepare for everything." Dr. Stewart placed a hand over hers to settle them. "Just be open and honest. State the reasons why you contacted Wes, but don't blame her for the reason. Do you understand what I'm saying?"

"But she is to blame," Jade replied sharply. "I'm not talking about her PPD. I'm talking about the way she went about this before she had the embryos implanted. There was a string of bad decisions and it set off a chain reaction. Choosing Wes for starters. What if her kids got sexually involved with one of their cousins years from now? She lied to both Wes and me and said she used anonymous donors. And then the strain of three children at once. She said that was the doctor's idea… now I seriously wonder. I realize there are other mitigating factors, but I truly believe all of this contributed to her PPD."

"And it probably did."

"Thank you." Jade huffed. "I'll be honest…as much as I love my sister, I'm a little angry. My business in Los Angeles is suffering because I'm not there. If she had come to me, I could have moved her out there temporarily and gotten her the help she needed. I think my sister has been a little selfish."

"Millie," Dr. Stewart said. "Set up a few counseling sessions between Liv and Jade. Let's say three for now, the first one today."

"Do you want it before or after she sees the children?"

"Ah." Dr. Stewart pursed her lips and tilted her head from side to side. "After. I want her to be distraction free when she's with her daughters." Dr. Stewart returned her attention to Jade. "We're going to ask Liv to come in, you two can catch up a little, then we'll ask you to leave for an hour or two. We have a Families Dealing with PPD seminar at eleven o'clock if you're interested. I think you'll find it very informative. Families eat together on Sunday, then we'll regroup in the afternoon and you and Liv will have a session together."

"Okay." Jade mentally ran through her list of things to do. She'd left in the middle of Delta and Garrett's wedding. She still needed to do teardown, on top of readying the linens and other rented items so they could be returned to their vendors. Never mind all she had to do for her own business.

Dr. Stewart nodded to Millie. "We're ready for Liv."

Jade ran her hands over her jeans, not knowing what to expect from her sister. Liv appeared in the doorway, dressed casually in a pair of khaki shorts, a white cotton T-shirt and tennis shoes. Her eyes darted from Jade to the girls and back again. While she looked healthy, her cheeks appeared hollower than they had been when Jade had last seen her. The high ponytail only accentuated her weight loss. She didn't look like someone who'd carried triplets two months ago.

"It's good to see you." Jade rose from the couch and crossed the room to her. "I've missed you. And I love you."

"I love you more." The corners of Liv's mouth lifted slightly at their familiar words. "You must think I'm a terrible person."

"Absolutely not." Jade held her sister's hands between her own, uncertain if a hug would be too much, too soon. "I think triplets are a bit overwhelming for a single, first-time mom. It's impossible to do it all alone."

"How are you managing?" Liv asked, careful to avoid looking in the girls' direction.

"I have a small team helping me."

"A team?"

Jade sucked in her breath. She'd said too much. "Maddie at night and a couple of sitters during the day. Like you had talked about hiring a nanny once you returned from maternity leave. That's what I've done. I need to work, so I have someone there with me almost all the time to help. I can't do it alone."

"I guess that makes me feel a little better." Liv's face began to brighten. "Who did you get? I had a tough time finding a qualified nanny to take on triplets."

"They're babysitters. Not nannies. There's two of them."

"Who are they?" Liv's eyes narrowed slightly. "What aren't you telling me?"

Why weren't Dr. Stewart or Millie intervening? "They're two local teens. Emma Slade uses them and sings their praises." Jade didn't see the need to add that Wes had referred them to her.

"Slade?" Liv dropped her hands and took a step backward. "What did you do?"

"I uncovered the girls' paternity while I was trying to figure out where you ran off to." There, Band-Aid off. It's out in the open.

"Oh no." Liv covered her mouth with her hands. "Do they know?"

Jade shook her head. "Only Wes does. And he knows I'm their biological mother." She looked at Dr. Stewart. "Is this okay?"

The woman nodded. "It's not how I would have preferred, but it's okay as long as you both continue to communicate effectively."

"Do you have feelings for Wes?" Jade asked.

"No, of course not." Liv's face twisted. "We were just friends."

"According to him, you were good friends. How would that have worked if he had stayed in town?"

"He wasn't staying in town. He talked about leaving constantly. I knew he was leaving before he did. It just would have been nice if he had said goodbye before taking off. That hurt."

"Help me understand something." Jade mentally rehearsed her words before speaking, not wanting to offend Liv. "Why did you choose a man who comes from

Saddle Ridge's largest family to father your children? His brothers have kids close in age. They'd be sitting with, playing with, and possibly even attracted to a relative and they wouldn't know it. I'm having a difficult time understanding your rationale."

"I planned on using a donor. Even after I asked Wes, I still leaned toward one."

"Why did you change your mind?"

"You and I kept having those conversations about medical history and what if something happened to the girls and they needed a donor for whatever reason. You just said it… Wes has a huge family of possible matches. I wouldn't have that with an anonymous donor. I took the risk of losing a great friend in exchange for my children's future health. Especially after watching one of my best friends battle cancer this year. I figured no one would know there was a family connection unless there was a medical crisis. And I would have dealt with it then. It wasn't until after the babies were born and Belle had Travis that I realized one of the girls might want to date him. Garrett moved to town with his children after I was already pregnant. The idea that of one of the girls might want to date his son one day terrified me. It was too late at that point. I just wanted my children to have options. I don't regret that part. When Wes and I first discussed this, there weren't any Slade children in town with the exception of Ivy, and she was seven at the time. The chance of them interacting was slim. Regardless, I regret not being more prepared for the what-ifs."

"Liv, you couldn't have been more prepared. You

knew everything there was to know about having children except the emotional aspect of it and I don't think anyone can ever prepare for that. What about Kevin? Did you think he'd come back once you had the children?"

"Kevin." Liv sighed. "He was my one true love. A part of me will always love him, but I knew he wasn't coming back. Even if he wanted to, I doubt I could ever trust him not to walk out on me again. Besides, he's engaged to be married soon."

"I heard all about it. You're okay with that?" Jade didn't want to bring up the fact she knew Kevin was marrying a woman with children. She assumed her sister already knew.

"It doesn't involve me." Liv's lips thinned and Jade sensed a renewed tension in her words.

"If you weren't in love with Wes, why did you follow him all over the place?"

"Oh, for heaven sake, I wasn't following him." Liv threw her head back and laughed. "Have you seen some of those rodeo cowboys? Those men are hot. I wasn't interested in anyone around town, so I met up with Wes when it was convenient. I enjoyed the atmosphere. I enjoyed getting out of town for a day or two. And I certainly enjoyed the eye candy. So let me reiterate one more time, I'm not in love or attracted to Wes. Are you asking about Wes because you're interested in him?"

Jade opened her mouth and quickly shut it. She didn't want to lie to her sister. She didn't want to hurt her, either.

"Oh wow." Liv paled. "You and Wes. I never saw that coming."

"There is no me and Wes. He's gone and he doesn't plan on returning."

"Ever?"

"That was the original plan, wasn't it?" Jade's defenses began to rise. "You knew he was leaving town, that's why you used him as a donor. How could he possibly come back? It was extremely difficult for him to see the girls." Liv had been in the room with the girls for ten minutes and she still hadn't touched, hugged or even looked their way for longer than a second.

"It sounds like he spent a lot of time with them." Liv's voice remained even and Jade couldn't get a read on her emotion.

"He was a great help to me."

"Liv," Dr. Stewart said. "How do you feel about Wes spending time with your daughters?"

"I don't like it." Liv held Jade's gaze. "She can have any man in the world, just not the father of my children."

Jade inhaled deeply, trying to collect her thoughts. "You should have told me you weren't using a donor. Wes and I have a history."

"You what?"

"We dated in high school. It was brief, but it didn't end well. You would have known that if you had told me you were fertilizing my eggs…with someone from town. Especially someone my age. Didn't you think the likelihood we went to school together was pretty high?"

"All the times I talked about you, Wes never once mentioned knowing you." Liv's voice broke as her hurt turned to anger.

"Because he hated me. We did some terrible things

to each other back then. But that doesn't matter now. I had a right to know. You violated our agreement and you violated my trust."

"Okay." Dr. Stewart crossed the room to stand between them. "Jade, you're blaming Liz."

"I don't know how to do this and not blame her." She glared at her sister. "This part happened before her postpartum depression. Honestly, Liv, your actions have terrified me. I'm still trying to figure out why you packed away all the girls' things in the downstairs closet?"

"I needed normalcy. I felt myself spinning out of control and I thought I could regain it if I confined everything baby to the two nurseries." Liv's face reddened in anger. "Clearly it didn't work. And despite whatever you feel you're entitled to, I was under no obligation to tell you who I chose to father my children."

"Our legal agreement says you were going to fertilize my eggs with an anonymous donor. Are you really going to split hairs and say it was anonymous to me and not to you? I think any court would frown on that."

"Oh, so now you want to take me to court?"

"I'm not saying that at all." Jade forced herself to stay calm despite her flaring temper beneath the surface. "Wes and I are the same age and we grew up in the same town. The chances were pretty high we knew each other. The point I'm trying to make is, I may have given you my eggs, but I still had certain rights. You should've told me what you were doing."

"You're right. I had blinders on all through this. I was so excited about finally having a family of my own, I didn't take anyone else's feelings into consideration."

"There is something else I need to tell you."

Liv's body went rigid, bracing herself for another onslaught. "I'm listening."

"I've been living at Silver Bells with the girls in one of the larger family guest cabins."

"You took my children out of their home? Why?"

"Because Maddie and I couldn't do it alone. I am so grateful she offered to stay with me but she has a job and a life of her own. I think you may have forgotten I have a business to run, and it's been difficult to do long-distance. The two girls that babysit for me live on the ranch. It's very convenient for me to stay there."

"I bet," Liv said sarcastically. "Don't you find it a bit hypocritical? You just finished preaching to me about the girls growing up in the same town with their cousins and all these what-if scenarios...yet you have them all living on the same ranch."

"They're infants. They don't know what a cousin or even a relative is. I think there's a difference. If it makes you uncomfortable, I will move back to your house. I only went to the ranch because I needed all the help I could get. I didn't do it to hurt you. I did it for their safety and well-being. If there was a fire, I wouldn't even be able to get the three of them out of the house at the same time. This way there is usually two people watching the girls."

"I'm not asking you to leave. I gave you temporary guardianship because I trust you. So I have to trust you're making the right decisions." Liv crossed the room to her daughters. "With so many people around, they probably don't even miss me."

"They have definitely missed you."

"How do you know?" Liv said in a broken whisper.

"Because they're never settled. Not completely. They always seem to be looking for someone."

"Really?" Liv glanced back at Jade. "You're not just saying that?"

"No, I mean it. You're their mom and they love you."

"But I left."

"You left to get help." Jade wondered if the guilt Molly had told her about was what Liv was experiencing now. "They don't feel the same way toward you that we felt toward Mom. It's different, Liv."

"Thank you. I needed to hear that."

"It's the truth." Jade moved to stand beside her. "I have something funny to tell you." She nudged Liv's arm. "When I first got to your house, I was so afraid I'd mix them up, I wrote their first initials on the bottom of their feet."

Liv tried to suppress a laugh. "You did what? They're not identical."

"All babies look alike to me." Jade shrugged. "I used permanent marker so it wouldn't wash off when I gave them a bath."

"No, you didn't!" Liv said, half laughing, half crying. "Do their little feet still have writing on them?"

"No. It eventually wore off." Jade smiled, relieved to see her sister in good humor. "See, they're very intrigued by you. And I think Audra has your eyes."

"I can't believe how much they've grown in such a short time." Hadley brought her tiny hand to her mouth and smiled up at her mother. "Oh my God, they're smiling now."

"I'm still trying to figure out if it's a genuine smile or gas. They've been a little stinky. They have their two-month checkup on Tuesday so I'll ask the pediatrician about it."

"It's probably the formula again." Liv's shoulders slumped. "I thought the last one was the right one. It would have been so much easier if I had been able to breast-feed them."

"Liv," Dr. Stewart interrupted. "Remember what we talked about. Your inability to breast-feed was not your fault."

Liv nodded and knelt on the floor in front of them. Jade was glad to see her sister interact with the girls, but it also meant her time with them would soon end. That's what she wanted, wasn't it? Then why did it hurt?

"I'm going to head out for a little while and give you some time with them."

Liv smiled at her over her shoulder. "Thank you for coming today."

"Anything for you."

BY THE TIME Jade locked the car seats into their bases in the back of the SUV, she felt physically and emotionally drained. She slid behind the wheel, turned the key in the ignition and switched on the AC to cool the vehicle down since it had been parked in the sun all day long. The clock on the dashboard glowed quarter to four. No wonder she was tired. She'd been going since two in the morning.

"Oh shoot!" Jade dug through her bag for her phone. "I forgot Tomás."

She flicked off the side mute button and tapped at the screen. Thirty-two missed calls, nine of which were from Tomás, twenty-seven text messages and over a hundred emails.

Nothing from Wes.

It wasn't like she had expected him to call. She said she'd call him later and she would once she got home. She glanced at the clock again. He was probably mid-flight, and if she called him now, she could get away with leaving a voice mail. It would be easier on them both after this morning's emotional goodbye.

She pulled up his contact and pressed Call. Straight to voice mail as she figured.

"Hi, Wes, it's Jade. It's almost four and I'm just leaving the PPD center. Liv saw the girls, but it was extremely slow going. After about half an hour, she got very overwhelmed. The doctor feels she'll probably need to be there for longer than thirty days. I told her that I knew about you and that you had spent time with the girls. I also let her know we were living on the ranch. She was upset at first, but she understood. Okay, um, well, I just wanted you to know, so I'll talk to you when I talk to you, I guess. I—I miss you, Wes. I'm sorry it had to be this way."

Jade disconnected the call. Maybe she shouldn't have told him the last part. Maybe she should have said more. No. It was better this way. She shifted the SUV into drive when her phone rang. Tomás.

She answered the call. "Hey, I'm sorry. I'm just getting ready to head home from the postpartum depression center, can I call you back when I get there?"

"I hope that means you're sitting down, because we have a problem."

Jade shifted back into Park. "Tell me."

"We lost the Wittingfords."

Jade gripped the phone tighter. "Lost as in they canceled or lost as in they went with someone else?"

"They went with someone else."

"No, no, no." Jade rested her head on the steering wheel. "What happened?"

"Word has gotten around that you're not in town and our competition is poaching our clients."

"But the Wittingfords have been with us for years. Their parties are the cornerstone of our business. Who did they go with?"

"Margot Schultz."

Oh no, not Margot. She was smart, savvy and had a world-class reputation. She was one of the best, if not the best, in the industry. "If she managed to take them, there's no telling who else she'll get. She has the potential to destroy us."

"When are you coming back? I can do a lot of things, but I'm not you."

"I don't know. Liv's first visit with the girls did not go well. And they're telling me she'll be there past thirty days. Possibly sixty or ninety days."

"Wow, love, I'm so sorry to hear that. I still don't understand why you can't check her into a facility here."

"If I had known about this in advance, I would have. She's comfortable where she is and it seems like a great place. I just have to do the best I can from here." She turned in the seat to make sure the girls weren't too cold. "I know you're trying to find the perfect candidate, but I want you to hire two people by tomorrow afternoon. No exceptions, Tomás. I refuse to lose my business because you're picky. You can train whoever you need to train and mold them into mini yous. If you think you need to hire three people, then do it. But I need you to be me. Your reputation in this town is just as good as mine. There is nothing I can do that you can't."

"I appreciate the confidence you have in me, but—"

"But what? Is it money? Is that what you want? More money? I've already given you a raise, but if that's what it takes—"

"Jade, breathe," Tomás ordered. "I was going to say, it's not the same without you here. I miss you, love."

"I miss you too. And thank you. It's nice feeling wanted."

"Uh-oh, problems with your cowboy?"

"He flew home to Texas today."

"And are you okay with that?" Tomás asked.

"I haven't had time to think about it. Dwelling on what could never be is an exercise in futility. We spent some time together, we shared a few kisses and that was all it could ever be. After the way Liv reacted today when I told her Wes was in the girls' lives, I feel even more guilty."

"Whoa, I'll let you tell me about the kisses later, but you two shared a lot more than that. You have children together. Donor or not, you're always going to be connected. I can only imagine that loss. And we don't have to talk about it. You can choose to ignore it all you want, just know, I'm here for you if you need a shoulder to lean on."

More like cry on. Jade missed Wes. Watching him walk out the door hurt more than losing her biggest client. She hung up and steered the SUV onto the highway. She had Tomás, Maddie, everyone on the ranch and she had the girls, yet she'd never been more alone. She did feel a loss. Whether she wanted to or not, she had fallen hard for the cowboy. Her sister was right. She could have any man in the world…just not Wes.

Chapter Ten

The warm Texas sun felt good on his shoulders as Wes strode across the Bridle Dance Ranch's parking lot toward the Ride 'em High! Rodeo School's outdoor arena.

"Oh, I know that look," Shane Langtry said from the top fence rail as a teenage version of him demonstrated technique in the center of the ring. "Either you just got bad news or you just got your heart broken."

"What are you, clairvoyant?" Wes watched Shane's son execute a smooth dismount after a successful eight second ride. Something he may never do again. "Hunter looks good out there."

"Thanks. I have no doubt he'll take the championship one day." Shane swung his legs over the fence and jumped down. "Well, am I right?"

"About Hunter? Most definitely. He's the finest young rider I've ever seen."

"I'm asking if I was right about you."

"Yeah, a little."

"From the expression on your face I'd say whatever's on your mind is more than a little. Did you see Dr. Lindstrom?"

"I'm just returning from there. Thank you for the referral. She's really nice, although I didn't want to hear what she said."

"You know who she's married to, don't you?" Shane pushed his hat back and propped an arm on the fence.

"No, who?"

"Brady Sawyer."

"*The* Brady Sawyer? The Brady Sawyer who works here?" The man had been a legend on the circuit until an accident paralyzed him from the waist down. They never thought he'd walk again, but he not only walked, he went on to compete until he retired. Now he works helping others to recover at Dance of Hope, the nonprofit hippotherapy center Shane's mother owned next door. "I had no idea."

"She was one of his doctors who put him back together. They fell pretty hard for each other while he was recuperating. If she could fix him, she can fix you. What did she say?"

"She confirmed what my first doctor had suspected." Wes watched another teen climb into the chute, remembering back to when he was that age. He thought he was invincible. If he got bucked off he just shook it off and got right back on. "There's no way I can compete again unless I have the surgery. And then I'm looking at six months to a year recovery."

"So it's not a matter of if you're going to have the surgery, it's when you'll have it."

"It's scheduled a week from today. Next Wednesday." Wes hadn't even told his agent yet. As much as he had wanted to wait, the pain had become too intense. If it meant his biggest sponsors not renewing his contracts this year, then so be it. He would just have to work twice as hard next year. He'd been debating his options since his last competition. While the surgery alone terrified him, not doing what he loved most terrified him more. "That will leave me without a job though. I won't be able to teach for a while. I guess I'm giving you notice since I can't expect you to keep my position open for that long. But don't worry, I have enough money to cover my rent here on the ranch."

"You're just Mr. Doom-and-Gloom today, aren't you?" Shane gripped Wes's good shoulder. "You need to relax, man. I can temporarily fill your position until you are able to come back to work, however long that takes."

"Thank you."

Wes had feared his only other option would be to move back home and partner with his brothers at Silver Bells, if they still wanted him. After the other day, he never wanted to step foot in Saddle Ridge again. He couldn't risk running into Jade or the girls. She updated him daily through voice mail and text messages and that was enough for him. But Harlan had asked him to be his best man at his and Belle's renewal ceremony, so he had to go back. Why did they have to get married again, anyway?

"There's something I want to run by you. I've been tossing the idea around for a while, but I haven't found the right person to help me with it. Your extensive recovery time may work to both of our advantages."

"Sounds intriguing. What do you have in mind?"

"Between rodeo clinics and my son's competitions

I'm on the road a lot. I really need a rodeo school director and if you're interested, I think we can work something out. It would be full-time, more money and full benefits."

"Seriously?" The deal seemed almost too good to be true. "I've only been here six months. Are you sure you don't want to choose someone else?"

"I think you're the best fit. You've shown an interest in the business side of things and that's what I need. Somebody who can see the business beyond today. Walk with me." Shane motioned for Wes to follow him down the wide path leading toward the Bridle Dance Ranch's stables. The quarter-million-acre estate housed three of Hill Country's most successful businesses, including one of the state's largest paint and cutting horse ranches. "Between running the ranch and the rodeo school with my brothers, I can't do everything I need or even want to do. You'd be helping me immensely. And I don't know how much thought you've given to retirement, but you always need to have something lined up past today in case an injury sidelines you. This will give you that opportunity to compete for another year or two after you've recovered and have something solid to fall back on."

"I'd say that sounds like an offer I can't refuse." Wes held out his hand. "Thank you."

Shane shook on it and laughed. "I'll take this as a tentative yes. I want you to really mull it over and get through your surgery before you give me your final answer. From what I understand those initial few weeks after a rotator cuff repair can be pretty painful. You're privileged to have access to some of the best physical therapists and nursing staff here on the ranch. Don't hesitate to ask for help."

"Thank you. I knew moving here was the best decision I ever made."

"Just do me one favor. Don't accept the job because you're running away from that broken heart you're trying to hide. You asked me earlier if I was clairvoyant so don't try to deny it. I've been there, done that and then some. If you have something unresolved with your woman, you owe it to both of you to see it through."

"There's nothing left to resolve." Wes's mind still burned with the final images of Jade and the girls. Despite the love he had for them, he wouldn't—couldn't—go through that pain again. "It's over."

Jade froze at the sight of Emma and Belle pushing their baby carriages down the road toward the cabin. She had just returned from her second family day at the postpartum depression treatment center and hadn't even had the chance to get the girls inside. She fumbled with the latch release on Mackenzie's car seat, trying desperately to separate it from the base.

"Need some help?" Harlan's wife asked. Without waiting for an answer, she opened the door on the other side of the SUV and released Audra's car seat. "They are so adorable. I never get a chance to see them."

Mackenzie's seat finally popped free. "I know. Between your schedule and my schedule—" *and the fact I'm trying to hide the girls' paternity from your fam-*

ily "—we keep missing each other. We just came from visiting Liv."

"Here, I'll take her." Emma startled Jade as she reached for the car seat's handle.

Jade snatched it back. "Would you be able to get Hadley instead? This one has a dirty diaper I need to change."

"Sure."

Jade quickly climbed the porch stairs and shoved her key in the lock. She needed to get Mackenzie out of sight as quickly as possible. The whole "hide the baby" routine had worn thin and a part of her wished the truth would come out now. Because regardless of what Wes and Liv wanted, it had to come out eventually. Whether on purpose or by accident it would happen one day and it was better for the girls if it happened before they were old enough to understand what was going on.

Jade sat the car seat next to the changing table and unfastened Mackenzie. How could such a sweet, innocent child have so much drama surrounding her? She eased the infant into her arms, kissing the top of her sleepy head before laying her down. She unsnapped her pink-and-white unicorn pajamas and checked her diaper. Surprisingly, she didn't need a change. Ever since the pediatrician had switched their formula, the girls had been significantly less gassy and odiferous. Liv had been right. They were having a reaction to the formula and Jade had missed it.

"Do you need me to heat their bottles or anything?" Belle asked from the nursery doorway. "I'm exhausted just running around with one baby, never mind three."

"Um, actually, that would be great." Jade choked back the tears threatening to break free.

"Hey, what is it?" Belle wrapped an arm around her. "What happened?"

Jade shook her head, fearing she'd cry if she opened her mouth.

"It's okay." Belle pulled her into a hug. "This has to be so hard on you."

If she only knew all the reasons why.

"I'm sorry." Jade pulled away from her. "I'm just a little overwhelmed today. Of course it's nothing compared to my sister, so I just need to quit my complaining."

"How is Liv doing?"

"Better, but not great. Today was her third session with the girls. We went in the middle of the week for a brief visit, but on Sundays the residents spend the entire day with their children, including feeding and changing them. She's capable of doing that, but she worries she's doing it wrong. If she's with one child and the other starts crying, she feels guilty because she's not there for both of them or not doing something fast enough. She gets very overwhelmed with it and blames herself for everything."

"Wow, I can't imagine. I mean as a new mom I always wonder if I'm doing the right thing. Even with my animal rescue work, I'm constantly questioning myself."

"And that's normal." Jade finished changing Mackenzie's diaper and refastened her pajamas. "A lot of it is a hormonal imbalance and Liv refuses to take any medication. I respect her reasons for not wanting to, but it's delaying her progress."

"And the longer she's there, the more stress on you."

Jade didn't want to think that way. She was the only family her sister had and she needed to be there for her, regardless of the sacrifice. "I can't worry about me. I have to worry about her and the girls."

"You are allowed to worry about you. Let me tell you something. I don't feel the least bit guilty leaving Travis with Harlan so I can go out with my friends. Do I do it every night? Absolutely not. But every couple of weeks, I need a girls' night out. And Harlan and I need our date nights. That's the beauty of having family so close. We all watch each other's kids. In fact, you need to come out with us. Between Harlan, Garrett and Dylan, they are more than capable of watching the kids and you, me, Emma and Delta will go out."

"I wouldn't want to intrude on your family time." Nor did she think the Slade men could handle Audra, Hadley and Mackenzie at the same time.

"Honey, above all else, we're friends and friends support one another. Friends have dinner and drinks together. Besides, I don't think this one will mind you going out for a few hours." Belle smiled down at Mackenzie. "Hmm. I hadn't realized how much she looks like Travis."

"Really?" Jade held her breath. *I'm sorry, Liv.*

"Babies are funny that way." She trailed the back of her finger down Mackenzie's cheek. "I ran into a woman just last week at the pediatrician's office whose daughter looked identical to Holly. You would've sworn they were the same child."

"Wow." Jade tried not to show the relief leaving her body. "That had to have been unnerving."

"It was a little." Belle spun around and headed to the door. "I'll start on their bottles."

"I'm right behind you."

Just as soon as I pick myself up off the floor.

After she'd finally managed to get her pulse under control, Liv joined Emma and Belle in the living room. They already had the girls out of their carriers and on the play mats next to Emma and Travis.

This was why her sister and Wes needed to tell everyone the truth. Not only did Audra, Hadley and Mackenzie deserve to grow up knowing their extended family, Liv needed the companionship of other moms.

"I hear you're going to join us for girls' night this week."

"I'm considering it." Jade lowered Mackenzie to the play mat, burying any fear she had of the women discovering the baby's paternity. If the truth came out, it came out. She would deal with the fallout later. "I'm still trying to juggle everything in Los Angeles, although my assistant managed to bring in one of Hollywood's biggest producers. I'm not going to name names, but let's just say he has billions to spend."

"Oh! I know, I know." Emma raised Holly's little hand in the air. "Do you want to tell us or should we *phone home* for the answer?"

"I can't tell you that." Jade was barely able to keep the laughter from her voice. "At least not yet. Nothing is finalized—but fingers crossed—by tonight it will be."

"What kind of event is it?" Belle lifted Hadley in her arms and held the bottle to her lips.

"An award show after party." Jade grabbed a few towels from the kitchen and joined them on the floor. She placed Mackenzie in one of the chairs Wes gave them, tilted it back slightly so she could prop a towel under the bottle, allowing Mackenzie to drink on her own.

"Okay, now I'm jealous." Emma frowned. "That means you'll get to meet all the stars that night?"

"Would you guys hate me if I told you I've already met a lot of them?"

"No wonder you're anxious to get back to California," Belle said. "That makes what I was going to ask you kind of underwhelming."

Jade cradled Audra and offered her the third bottle. "Don't be silly. Go ahead and ask."

"Harlan and I are planning to renew our vows on August 1. Last year's wedding was a little rushed and unexpected. We didn't even have a chance to invite anyone. People heard about it through word-of-mouth and showed up, but it wasn't exactly our dream wedding. Our anniversary is on a Wednesday so we don't want a full-fledged wedding, but we want to have a really big party here at the ranch."

"Basically the wedding reception you never had."

"Exactly." Belle gently rocked back and forth on her knees as Hadley sucked happily on the bottle. Jade had always sat rigidly still while feeding them. "I was going to ask you for some ideas, because I know you're busy and I'd really like to plan this party with Harlan. We just want to make it special. Our track record with weddings isn't exactly the greatest."

"I'd be happy to help you."

"Really? Thank you. I have some ideas, but I'd like some professional input. And we'll pay you. I don't want you to think we're taking advantage of your knowledge."

"You'll do no such thing. Your family stepped in to help me in place of the family I don't have. I've never experienced that before. All of you have shown me a different side to family life. A happy side I wasn't sure existed."

"Does that mean you're ready to settle down and have children of your own? Because you and Wes would have beautiful kids."

Jade began to cough. "Wes and I—" She cleared her throat. "Wes and I are not a couple."

"You two sure looked like a couple at my wedding. That was some kiss." Emma winked.

"And sometimes a kiss is just a kiss."

"I call baby doody on that one," Belle laughed. "There is definitely something between you two and you'll have another chance to find out when he comes home for our ceremony. Harlan asked him to be his best man."

"Will he be able to fly so soon after surgery?" Emma asked.

"Surgery?" Jade looked from Emma to Belle. "What surgery?"

"I'm sorry, I thought you knew." Belle grimaced.

"Wes is having rotator cuff surgery on Wednesday. He'll be out of commission for six months to a year."

"I didn't realize he had made a decision already." Wes's shoulder must've gotten worse for him to abandon his plan to wait until the end of the season. "What is he going to do for work?"

"His boss in Texas offered him a director position," Belle answered. "But he's taking a few weeks to decide."

"I know Dylan wishes he would move home, but he's already offered him a partnership twice and he turned it down. It's a shame you and Wes both don't live here permanently." Emma stretched out on the floor next to her daughter. "Silver Bells and Saddle Ridge could really use an event planner. I don't mean just little small-time weddings like ours. We're surrounded by ski resorts and other large guest ranches that would benefit from your services. Plus, I think Wes would move here if you did."

"Can't you open a second location?" Belle asked. "Saddle Ridge can be your satellite office."

Leave Los Angeles? Even if she wanted to—and a small part of her was excited by the prospect of opening a second office—she couldn't. It would be great for her sister, but horrible for her. Saddle Ridge already held too many memories. And while she had made some sweet ones during this visit, it was just that…a visit. Saddle Ridge would never be home without Wes and there was no way he would ever move back.

Chapter Eleven

Wes knew it would be difficult seeing Jade after five weeks away, he just hadn't expected her to take his breath away when he did. He'd managed to avoid her during Harlan and Belle's vow renewal, but once the reception was in full swing, he found her repeatedly in his line of vision. And what a vision she was. Her vintage cream-and-pale-pink dress caused his heart to flutter. And nothing on a man should ever flutter.

Despite his family's best attempts to get them together, Wes and Jade had managed to stay on opposite sides of the wood plank dance floor. The sun had just begun to set and he finally understood the meaning of the phrase *golden hour*. It was as if an ethereal light shone upon her, making him long for the kisses they had once shared.

Wes shook his head and reached into the front pocket of his jeans and pulled out his prescription bottle. "What the hell did they put in these things?" Dr. Lindstrom had renewed his painkillers before his flight despite his protests. He was glad she had. The cabin pressure and change in altitude had bothered his shoulder to the point he'd had to take one earlier that day. It should've worn off by now.

"Have you given any more thought to our offer?" Garrett handed him a bottle of Coke. He would've much rather preferred a beer or two, but he didn't want to chance mixing alcohol with his meds. "It's a serious offer, Wes. We don't want you to think it's out of pity."

"I know it's not. And I appreciate it, but I just can't move back here. It's too hard."

"Believe me, I totally understand. I felt the same way before I moved back. I saw Dad on every street corner. Everywhere I turned…he was there. Now that I've been home for a while, other memories, new memories, have taken their place. When I walked past the feed and grain, I don't see Dad with the sack of feed over his shoulder. I see Bryce racing through the door to see the baby chicks they have in the back. Just like when I used to go to the Iron Horse for dinner, I saw Rebecca and me on the dance floor." Garrett swallowed hard at the memory of his deceased wife.

"I know you did." Wes slung an arm around his brother's shoulder feeling the distance close between them for the first time in years.

"The point I'm trying to make is you can create new memories. Now when I walk in there, I still see Rebecca, but I also see my first date with Delta."

Wes wanted desperately to confide in his brother. To tell him exactly why he couldn't move home. He loved his brothers. And as their families grew, he had more people to love. But it wasn't enough to make him stay. The love he desperately wanted would never be his.

"I still want you to consider it. Please give us the same courtesy you're giving your job offer in Texas. Look at all the pros and cons. And talk to us. Every time I see you, you seem more distant. Let me tell you something, life is short. No one knows that better than me. You remember that. We are your family and we love you." Garrett took a step to the side. "I believe this lovely woman is waiting to speak with you."

Wes turned around to see Jade standing there. It reminded him of the first time he saw her when she came back to town. Only a month and a half had passed since then, but it seemed like a lifetime ago. He wanted to ask his brother to stay and tell Jade he had nothing more to say, but he needed something from her and it couldn't wait.

"Hi," Jade said.

"Hi," Wes replied.

"Oh, come on. Please tell me you two have progressed further than this over the past couple months." Garrett placed a hand on both their shoulders. "I have an idea…try to com-mun-i-cate with one another. Take it from an old pro like me. It'll get you places." He winked and walked away.

"How have you been?" Jade absentmindedly twisted the ring on her middle finger. "Emma and Belle told me about your surgery. I tried to call you, but I always get your voice mail."

"I got your messages and thank you." Wes had wanted to return her calls, but self-preservation had come first.

"Why didn't you call me back?"

"Because talking to you...texting you...looking at you now just reminds me of what I'll never have. I didn't want a family or to settle down, yet that's all I can think about. You complicated my life."

Jade's eyes blazed. "I complicated your life? Oh no, no. You did that on your own when you went along with my sister's plan."

"Your sister's plan didn't involve me falling in love with you."

Dammit. He hadn't meant to say the words. He tried not to even think them. But they were there, every day at the forefront of his mind.

"Wes, I—"

"I need to see Liv." Wes purposely cut her off not wanting to hear that she didn't love him in return. "I tried calling the treatment center, at least the one that I think she's at, but she's never called me back."

"They're not allowed to talk on the phone. They have computer and email privileges along with old-fashioned snail mail, but most of their communication takes place in person and is supervised."

"Sounds more like prison."

"I wasn't a fan of it myself at first, but I've gotten used to it over the past five weeks."

"I take it things are improving." Wes kept hoping Liv would see that moving to California was best for all of them and leave Saddle Ridge for good. No Jade, no triplets, no heartbreak.

"Definitely. She'd even had a few overnight visits with them and while they were difficult, they went well. She'll be ready to come home soon, and then I'll head back to California. Out of all the crap I've been through in my life, that will be the hardest. I never wanted children and now that I've been caring for them, I don't want to give them up." Jade held up her hands. "I know, I know. I'm perfectly aware that they're not mine to keep, even though they are mine."

"They're ours." Wes wanted to hold her, to console her, but any touch would be too much to bear. "I want to talk to Liv. I need answers."

"I can tell you exactly what she said." Jade's tone flattened.

Wes sensed an argument about to erupt if he wasn't careful. "I need to hear them from her. We were each other's confidants. She was my best friend and there were a lot of times I was closer to her than to them. We owe it to each other."

"I will call the center in the morning and see if I can get it approved. If they say yes, you can come with us on Friday."

"'Us' as in you and the girls?" How could she still not get it?

"Yes."

"No. I can't see them again." His heart squeezed at the thought alone. "Please respect that. I appreciate you keeping me updated, I hope you never stop doing that, but I can't continue to talk to you."

"So that's how it's going to be? You tell me you love me and then nothing. What is there, then?"

"Nothing. There's nothing. There can never be anything more than that unless…" Wes couldn't say the words out loud. He couldn't risk his heart turning to dust in case Liv refused to allow him to be a part of the girls' lives. The chance was small, but he had to try. "I fly home on Saturday. Please let me know when I can see her."

"Fine." Jade stiffened her spine, her face a bright shade of pink. "I'll text you. Don't worry, I don't expect a reply."

She spun away from him and stormed across the dance floor, almost taking out a couple in the process. He'd rather she be mad at him than hurt. He'd take anger over heartbreak any day.

WES HADN'T EXPECTED Liv to meet with him so soon, if at all. After meeting with her counselor and physician, a woman named Millie escorted him to a sitting area that reminded him of his old living room at Silver Bells.

When she walked in, he was surprised by how great she looked. He hadn't known what to expect, but based on what Jade had told him, he assumed she'd either be in a hospital gown or some sort of a uniform.

"You look fantastic." Wes took a step closer to give her a hug, then froze when she crossed her arms. "No? Okay. I gotcha." He cleared his throat. "So, um how does this work?"

"You talk to me like I'm a human being."

Liv's words smacked him like a hot tuna on a grill. "Haven't I always?"

"I thought you moved to Texas. What are you doing here and what happened to your arm?"

"Harlan and Belle renewed their wedding vows so I'm here for that and I had to have rotator cuff surgery."

Concern flashed in her eyes. "What does that mean for your career? When will you be able to compete again?"

"Hopefully by next season. I'm being cautiously optimistic and realistic at the same time. I may be forced to retire early."

"What are you going to do?" Liv sank onto the couch across from him.

"I have a few options." Wes sat in the chair in front of her. "The rodeo school I work at in Texas offered me a director position that would still give me the time to compete if I'm able to."

Liv's shoulders dropped slightly. "That sounds like a nice opportunity."

"It's not the only offer on the table. My brothers asked me to partner with them again." Wes watched Liv's left eye twitch ever so slightly as she white-knuckle-gripped her thighs. Now it made sense. She wasn't concerned about his well-being. She wanted to make sure he wasn't moving home.

"So you haven't decided yet?"

"I'm leaning in one direction, but I promised my brothers and my job in Texas that I would take the next couple of weeks to think it over. It's a big decision." Wes inhaled deeply. "I didn't come here to talk about that. I came here because when I agreed to father your children, you told me you were using an anonymous egg donor. I would like to know why you didn't tell me the truth."

"I told Jade all of this."

"I haven't spoken to Jade other than asking to meet

with you. You and I were best friends. I think I'm owed some sort of an explanation."

"And I was owed a goodbye."

Hurt registered in her eyes. He had known their friendship would end, but he never meant to hurt her in the process.

"I couldn't say goodbye to you, Liv. If I saw you… pregnant with my children, I was afraid I'd want to be a part of their lives. It was better for both of us if I just left and told you afterward."

"Now that you've seen them, you do want to be in their lives?"

"Most definitely."

Liv inhaled sharply at his admission.

"But I know I can't be, despite my love for them. Unless for some reason you've changed your mind." He had hoped to ask her more delicately, but no matter how he chose to do it, he feared she'd see him as a threat.

"Why, because you're dating my sister? That was inappropriate. You knew she was the biological mother and you put the moves on her."

"For starters, I did not put the moves on Jade. Second, your sister and I are not dating, and third, my attraction to her grew out of the bond we have over those children and the concern for your well-being."

"You're telling me the kids and I are the reason you're attracted to my sister." Liv rolled her eyes, her voice heavy with sarcasm.

"I'm telling you it was an impossible situation. I'm not blaming you. I just want to know why you didn't tell me the truth."

"Because I was afraid you'd say no. I had an anonymous donor picked out. He was perfect on paper. Except he was as cut and dry as Jade and I are, meaning there was no family to fall back on in case my children got sick one day."

"I don't understand, you mean if something happened to you and Jade?"

"No, like if they needed a kidney or bone marrow transplant. I know it sounds illogical, but I've read so many things about donors being hard to find and children who die because they were on a waiting list for years. I wanted to make sure my daughters were covered for everything so they can have the best possible life. And if that time ever came, God forbid, I would have told the girls and your family the truth."

Wes leaned forward. "I just wish you had been open and honest with me. I wasn't just an anonymous donor from the fertility clinic. I was your friend and I had a right to know who I was creating a child with, even though I signed my other rights away, I did still have that right."

"It wasn't the perfect plan I thought it was. It's taken me a while to realize how selfish my actions were." Liv pushed her shoulders back and stared directly at him. "I realize I was wrong. I apologize, and I hope one day you can forgive me."

"Apology accepted. That doesn't change how I feel about Audra, Hadley and Mackenzie."

"They're my children and I decide who is and isn't in their lives. You were so determined to move away from Saddle Ridge, I knew you were leaving when I chose you. I always knew Jade would be a part of their lives. She's their aunt. But I can't have both of you involved or involved with each other."

"Why not?"

Liv ignored his question. "I thought you were dead set against having children."

"I've changed my mind." Wes stumbled for a way to explain it to her. "It's like the couple who has the wild hookup and the woman gets pregnant. Just because the guy never planned on having kids doesn't mean now that he has one on the way that he doesn't love his child."

"You're conveniently leaving a few factors out. You knew what you were doing at the time, so the fact that I was carrying your children wasn't a surprise. And then there's Jade. What do you think it does to me knowing the biological mother and the biological father of my children…the children I carried and gave birth to, are in love with each other?"

"Who said anything about love?" Wes couldn't believe for one second that Jade had emailed her sister and told her what he said last night.

"Sometimes you really are clueless. My sister's in love with you. I can see it in her eyes. I can see it every time she mentions your name, which thankfully isn't all that often. Your involvement with my sister makes me feel like an outsider with my own children. I can't have that. I've worked hard to recover from my postpartum depression. I haven't told my sister this yet, but they're releasing me tomorrow. I'm going to go home to my children and resume my life at my house. Not Silver Bells. I'm sorry, Wes, but I need you to honor our agreement. I don't want you in my daughters' lives."

Chapter Twelve

Sunny Southern California had never seemed so gloomy. Jade had been home for a month and despite trying her hardest, she still couldn't shake her Montana routine. She constantly checked her watch to see if it was time for the girls' feedings. She carefully listened to every sound in the middle of the night thinking one of them had woken up. And she hugged her pillow tight as she lay alone in her bed, wishing Wes was by her side.

She wanted to fly to Texas and tell him how much she loved him. She should have said it the night he told her, but she had been so scared. She'd never said the words to anyone except her sister. Loving Wes meant hurting Liv. And her sister had been hurt enough.

The day Liv came home had been one of her proudest moments. Saying goodbye to Wes and leaving the ranch had been one of Jade's saddest. After two weeks with her sister and the girls, Liv sent her packing…in the nicest way possible. She had hired a full-time nanny and was receiving outpatient therapy. Jade had no doubt her sister would be a wonderful mother to the girls. It didn't make missing them any easier.

The doorbell rang and Jade forced a smile on her face as she crossed the cold marble foyer of her Hollywood Hills home. She had everything she'd ever wanted. Turned out it wasn't what she wanted, after all.

"Hello, love," Tomás said as she answered the door. "You look simply smashing tonight."

The epitome of tall, dark and handsome, her new business partner kissed both her cheeks and offered her his arm. "Shall we? I still can't believe Margot Schultz invited us to one of her parties."

"I still say she's up to something."

Jade had promoted her longtime assistant to partner when he began snagging Hollywood's wealthiest clientele. Despite losing some clients in the beginning, in the two months she had been gone, he took her business to immeasurable heights. Nobody deserved a promotion more than him. With the addition of their three new employees, Jade had a chance to step back and breathe a little.

"I think tonight's the night we'll find you Mr. Right," Tomás giggled as they slid into the limousine waiting at the curb. "Listen to me. I'm a poet."

"There is no such thing as Mr. Right." The only man who came close was gone forever. Jade's clutch vibrated in her lap. She pulled out her phone and tapped at the screen. "Liv sent me a text message."

"I hope it's another picture of those adorable girls." Tomás leaned closer as she opened the message.

Need you here...please come now.

"Oh my God." Jade covered her mouth and quickly dialed her sister.

"Driver," Tomás called up front as he typed wildly on his phone. "Turn the car around."

Please answer the phone, Liv. Please answer the phone. Voice mail. "She's not picking up."

"I'm booking you on the next flight out of here." Tomás gave her hand a quick squeeze before returning to his phone.

Jade frantically dialed Maddie. Again, voice mail. "What the hell is going on?"

"Driver…take us to LAX. It looks like there is only one flight and it's leaving in an hour. You're going to be on it."

Jade looked down at her black evening gown. "I'm not exactly dressed for the occasion." There was nothing like trying to get through airport security with strappy four-inch Christian Louboutin stilettos.

"At least they won't accuse you of concealing any weapons in that dress."

"Give me your jacket," Jade said as she tried her sister again. "Where can she be? She just sent me a text message."

She called Delta next. No answer. By the time she got on the plane and had to turn off her phone, she'd exhausted her Saddle Ridge contacts. "Something's not right."

EIGHT HOURS LATER, she swiped her credit card on the cab's handheld reader in front of her sister's house. "Thank you for getting me here so fast." She palmed him a fifty-dollar bill. It was the only cash she had left in her small clutch.

Gathering the hem of her dress in her hand, she climbed the porch stairs, careful not to break her neck. Just as she reached for the doorknob, Liv swung the door wide.

"It's about time you got here." Liv's eyes widened. "Wow! Where were you coming from in that dress?"

Jade pushed past her and down the hall to the first-floor nursery. "Where are the girls?"

"They're upstairs sleeping." Liv sucked in her lips. "Um… I need you to come into the living room."

"No." Jade stomped past her. "I need to see them." As she flew past the living room archway, a familiar cowboy hat caught her eye. She spun on her heels, twisting her ankle in the process. Before she had a chance to hit the hardwood floor, Wes wrapped his arm around her and pulled her hard to him. "Wh-what are you doing here?"

Wes stared down at her, his mouth inches above hers. "That's what I'd like to know."

"The girls…" Jade whispered, her mind reeling from the man holding her upright and the pain in her ankle.

"I've already checked on them. They're sleeping peacefully."

"You saw them? You physically saw that they're okay?"

"Yes."

Jade turned her head to demand answers from Liv, only her sister was gone. "What is going on?"

"I don't know." Wes helped Jade into the living room

and eased her onto the couch. "I got a text message last night telling me to come right away," he said as he unlaced her shoes. He held her calf as his eyes trailed up her thigh, exposed by the high slit in her gown. "That's some dress." He stopped just shy of her cleavage, closing his eyes and cursing under his breath. "I tried calling Liv and then Maddie, but no one answered."

"I even tried calling your sisters-in-law, but there was no answer there, either. I was about to call Harlan when I had to board the plane."

"I'm glad you didn't call the police," Liv said from the doorway, holding an ice pack and a towel. "That would have been awkward to explain, even though your family is well aware of why you're here."

"They're what?" Wes sat back on his haunches as Liv handed him the ice pack.

"Sorry about your ankle." Liv wrinkled her nose. "That wasn't part of the plan."

"What plan?" Jade and Wes said in unison.

"After you both left and I started getting out more with the girls, a lot of people came up to me and told me how you two made a lovely couple. Maddie had already been singing both of your praises, but she filled me in on all Wes had done for the girls. And then Delta came over, and Emma called." She nervously laughed. "And then it hit me…the family that I wanted was much bigger than me and the girls. It was you." She pointed at Jade. "And all of the Slades, including you, Wes."

The sun had just begun to rise and filter into the room as Liv rose from her chair and looked out the window. Was her sister having a relapse? Was that possible with PPD?

"Liv, sit next to me." Jade patted the couch. "Oh, that's cold." She jumped when Wes rested the ice pack against her ankle.

"It's already starting to swell." Wes held her foot firmly. "Liv, I can't tell if you're trying or not trying to tell us something, but my patience is wearing a little thin. When we last spoke, you told me you didn't want me in your daughters' lives. Now you're saying their family is my family. You didn't tell them, did you?"

"Well…" Liv gnawed her bottom lip. "Yes, I did. I felt I owed them the truth. My actions not only threw your lives into total chaos, it had the potential of hurting the girls and Wes's family in the future. I hadn't thought about the school issue, or that the girls and their cousins would be friends. I was laser focused on having a baby. In hindsight, that destroyed my marriage more than our inability to have children."

Jade felt Wes's grip tighten slightly on her foot. "Liv, I love that you did the right thing, but that was Wes's place to tell his family. Not yours."

Wes exhaled slowly and stood. "I'm not concerned that you told them. I'm more concerned with what comes next."

The front door opened, and Harlan poked his head in. "Is it okay for us to come in now?"

"What's going on?" Jade tugged on Wes's arm. "Help me up. What are they doing here?"

"I called them."

Wes slid his good arm under her and lifted Jade beside him. "I'm almost afraid to believe what this might mean," Wes whispered.

One by one, the entire Slade family filed into Liv's small living room.

"Thank you for coming. And, Jade and Wes, please forgive my little trickery. I didn't think you would come otherwise. Especially Wes." Liv walked over to him and held his face in her hands. "Dear Wes. I am so sorry for the way I treated you. You gave me the greatest gift in the world, and I was so cruel. You asked to be a part of their lives. And today I'm giving that to you." Liv cupped her sister under the chin. "To both of you."

"Liv," Jade sobbed. "What are you saying?" She knew her sister would never relinquish her rights to the girls. If that's what she was doing, then there was something seriously wrong. "Liv, please."

"I've already contacted my attorney and he will meet with us later today to explain in further detail, but…"

"Liv, no." Jade pulled her sister into her arms. "You can't. I won't let you. You love those girls." She didn't care what she had to give up in California, she'd stay by her sister's side every day and make sure she was okay.

"Jade, sweetheart." Liv soothed her hair. "Because I love them, I'm asking you to become de facto parents."

"De what?" Jade released her sister. "I don't understand."

"De facto parents. In Montana, a child or children can have more than two parents. You and Wes would assume day-to-day parental roles with me."

"This isn't a sister-wife thing, is it?" Wes asked.

"I think I might be able to explain this." Harlan

stepped forward. "If you two choose to reside here in Montana, and like Liv said, assume the day-to-day parenting of the girls alongside her, her attorney can petition the court to have you named de facto parents. Because you're their biological parents, you have an excellent chance a judge will sign off on it."

"And considering my father is the judge—" Belle winked "—your odds are pretty good. We took Liv to meet with him and he detailed everything that needed to happen in order for the court to grant the arrangement."

"You both have to live in Montana though," Dylan said. "That partnership is still open if you want it."

"And I still say Saddle Ridge needs an event planner," Emma added.

Jade blindly reached behind her for Wes's hand. She needed to feel his touch, to know she wasn't dreaming.

"And you need a place to all live that's not too sister-wifey." Garrett laughed. "We talked it over with Liv, and we have two side-by-side guest cottages on Silver Bells that we'd like to offer you. They need to be renovated, but—"

"But the sale of this place will more than pay for them," Liv said. "You two would have your space, and I would have mine. The girls would have both houses to call home."

Jade's heart hammered in her chest. "Liv, are you sure about this? You love this place."

"I love you more." Liv clasped her hands over theirs. "Do you two love each other?"

"Yes," Wes said as he wiped away a tear. "I love

those girls more than life itself." He started to laugh. "And I really wish I had use of both arms right now."

"Oh, Wes." Jade wrapped both of her arms around his waist and looked up at him "I've got you. And I love you."

"I love you too, with all that I am." He looked across the room to his family. "I love all of you. And, Liv, thank you. This means everything to me, but there's just one problem." He sighed heavily.

"What?" Jade pulled away from him. They were so close. How could he possibly back out now?

Wes lowered himself on one knee and took her hand in his. "I don't have a ring or some grand speech prepared, but I have a lifetime that I'd like to share with you and our crazy, unconventional family. That is if you'll marry me."

A wave of euphoria bubbled inside her. "Yes! Yes, I'll marry you!"

The shadows in her heart had finally disappeared and she was happy. Blissfully happy with the father of her children and a family to call her own.

* * * * *

We hope you enjoyed this story from
Harlequin® Western Romance.

Harlequin® Western Romance is coming to an end, but community, cowboys and true love are here to stay. Starting July 2018, discover more heartfelt tales of family and friendship from **Harlequin® Special Edition**.

Romance is for life, and these stories show that every chapter in a relationship has its challenges and delights and that love can be renewed with each turn of the page!

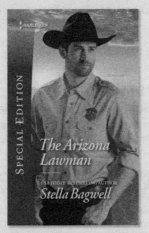

Look for six *new* romances every month from **Harlequin® Special Edition!**
Available wherever books are sold.

Get 4 FREE REWARDS!

We'll send you 2 FREE Books <u>plus</u> 2 FREE Mystery Gifts.

SPECIAL EDITION

A Kiss, a Dance & a Diamond

Helen Lacey

SPECIAL EDITION

Her Man on Three Rivers Ranch

Stella Bagwell

Harlequin® Special Edition books feature heroines finding the balance between their work life and personal life on the way to finding true love.

FREE
Value Over
$20

YES! Please send me 2 FREE Harlequin® Special Edition novels and my 2 FREE gifts (gifts are worth about $10 retail). After receiving them, if I don't wish to receive any more books, I can return the shipping statement marked "cancel." If I don't cancel, I will receive 6 brand-new novels every month and be billed just $4.99 per book in the U.S. or $5.74 per book in Canada. That's a savings of at least 12% off the cover price! It's quite a bargain! Shipping and handling is just 50¢ per book in the U.S. and 75¢ per book in Canada*. I understand that accepting the 2 free books and gifts places me under no obligation to buy anything. I can always return a shipment and cancel at any time. The free books and gifts are mine to keep no matter what I decide.

235/335 HDN GMY2

Name (please print)

Address   Apt. #

City   State/Province   Zip/Postal Code

Mail to the Reader Service:
IN U.S.A.: P.O. Box 1341, Buffalo, NY 14240-8531
IN CANADA: P.O. Box 603, Fort Erie, Ontario L2A 5X3

Want to try two free books from another series! Call 1-800-873-8635 or visit www.ReaderService.com.

HSE18

Looking for more satisfying love stories
with community and family at their core?

Check out **Harlequin® Special Edition**
and **Harlequin® Western Romance** books!

New books available every month!

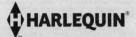